These Happy Golden Years

Other titles in the
Little House *on the* **Prairie** *series:*

LAURA INGALLS WILDER

These Happy Golden Years

EGMONT

EGMONT

We bring stories to life

First published in the USA 1943
First published in Great Britain 1963
by Lutterworth Press
This edition first published in 2015 by Egmont UK Limited
The Yellow Building, 1 Nicholas Road, London W11 4AN

Text copyright © 1943 HarperCollins
Cover illustration © 2015 Jonathan Burton
Inside illustrations © 1953 Garth Williams

ISBN 978 1 4052 8017 4

www.egmont.co.uk

A CIP catalogue record for this title is available from the British
Library

Printed and bound in Great Britain by the CPI Group

61178/1

Stay safe online. Any website addresses listed in this book are correct at the
time of going to print. However, Egmont is not responsible for content
hosted by third parties. Please be aware that online content can be subject
to change and websites can contain content that is unsuitable for children.
We advise that all children are supervised when using the internet.

MIX
Paper
FSC FSC® C018306

Contents

Laura Leaves Home

Sunday afternoon was clear, and the snow-covered prairie sparkled in the sunshine. A little wind blew gently from the south, but it was so cold that the sled runners squeaked as they slid on the hard-packed snow. The horses' hoofs made a dull sound, clop, clop, clop. Pa did not say anything.

Sitting beside him on the board laid across the bobsled, Laura did not say anything either. There was nothing to say. She was on her way to teach school.

Only yesterday she was a schoolgirl; now she was a schoolteacher. This had happened so suddenly, Laura could hardly stop expecting that tomorrow she would be going to school with little sister Carrie, and sitting in her seat with Ida Brown. But tomorrow she would be teaching school.

She did not really know how to do it. She never had taught school, and she was not sixteen years old yet. Even for fifteen, she was small; and now she felt very small.

The slightly rolling, snowy land lay empty all around. The high, thin sky was empty overhead. Laura did not look

1

back, but she knew that the town was miles behind her now; it was only a small dark blot on the empty prairie's whiteness. In the warm sitting room there, Ma and Carrie and Grace were far away.

Brewster settlement was still miles ahead. It was twelve miles from town. Laura did not know what it was like. She did not know anyone there. She had seen Mr Brewster only once, when he came to hire her to teach the school. He was thin and brown, like any homesteader; he did not have much to say for himself.

Pa sat looking ahead into the distance while he held the reins in his mittened hands and now and then chirruped to the horses. But he knew how Laura felt. At last he turned his face towards her and spoke, as if he were answering her dread of tomorrow.

'Well, Laura! You are a schoolteacher now! We knew you would be, didn't we? Though we didn't expect it so soon.'

'Do you think I can, Pa?' Laura answered. 'Suppose . . . just suppose . . . the children won't obey me when they see how little I am.'

'Of course you can,' Pa assured her. 'You've never failed yet at anything you tried to do, have you?'

'Well, no,' Laura admitted. 'But I . . . I never tried to teach school.'

'You've tackled every job that ever came your way,' Pa said. 'You never shirked, and you always stuck to it till you did what you set out to do. Success gets to be a habit, like anything else a fellow keeps on doing.'

Again there was a silence except for the squeaking of the sled runners and the clop-clop-clop of the horses' feet on the hard snow. Laura felt a little better. It was true; she always had kept on trying; she had always had to. Well, now she had to teach school.

'Remember that time on Plum Creek, Half-Pint?' Pa said. 'Your Ma and I went to town, and a blizzard came up? And you got the whole woodpile into the house.'

Laura laughed out loud, and Pa's laugh rang like great bells in the cold stillness. How little and scared and funny she had been, that day so long ago!

'That's the way to tackle things!' Pa said. 'Have confidence in yourself, and you can lick anything. You have confidence in yourself, that's the only way to make other folks have confidence in you.' He paused, and then said, 'One thing you must guard against.'

'What, Pa?' Laura asked.

'You are so quick, flutterbudget. You are apt to act or speak first, and think afterwards. Now you must do your thinking first and speak afterwards. If you will remember to do that, you will not have any trouble.'

'I will, Pa,' Laura said earnestly.

It was really too cold to talk. Snug enough under the heavy blankets and quilts, they went on silently towards the south. The cold wind blew against their faces. A faint trace of sled runners stretched onward before them. There was nothing else to see but the endless, low white land and the huge pale sky, and the horses' blue shadows blotting the sparkle from the snow.

The wind kept Laura's thick black woollen veil rippling before her eyes. Her breath was frozen in a patch of frost in the veil, that kept slapping cold and damp against her mouth and nose.

At last she saw a house ahead. Very small at first, it grew larger as they came nearer to it. Half a mile away there was another, smaller one, and far beyond it, another. Then still another appeared. Four houses; that was all. They were far apart and small on the white prairie.

Pa pulled up the horses. Mr Brewster's house looked like two claim shanties put together to make a peaked roof. Its tar-paper roof was bare, and melted snow had run into big icicles that hung from the eaves in blobby columns larger around than Laura's arms. They looked like huge, jagged teeth. Some bit into the snow, and some were broken off. The broken chunks of ice lay frozen into the dirty snow around the door, where dishwater had been thrown. There was no curtain at the window, but smoke blew from the stovepipe that was anchored to the roof with wires.

Mr Brewster opened the door. A child was squalling in the house, and he spoke loudly to be heard. 'Come in, Ingalls! Come in and warm yourself.'

'Thank you,' Pa replied. 'But it's a long twelve miles home and I'd better be going.'

Laura slid out from under the blankets quickly, not to let the cold in. Pa handed her Ma's satchel, that held her change of underclothes, her other dress, and her schoolbooks.

'Good-bye, Pa,' she said.

'Good-bye, Laura.' His blue eyes smiled encouragement to her. But twelve miles was too far to drive often; she would not see him again for two months.

She went quickly into the house. Coming from the bright sunshine, she could not see anything for a moment. Mr Brewster said, 'This is Mrs Brewster; and Lib, here's the teacher.'

A sullen-looking woman stood by the stove, stirring something in a frying pan. A little boy was hanging on to her skirts and crying. His face was dirty and his nose needed a handkerchief.

'Good afternoon, Mrs Brewster,' Laura said as cheerfully as she possibly could.

'Just go in the other room and take off your wraps,' Mrs Brewster said. 'Hang them behind the curtain where the sofa is.' She turned her back on Laura and went on stirring the gravy in the pan.

Laura did not know what to think. She could not have done anything to offend Mrs Brewster. She went into the other room.

The partition stood under the peak of the roof, and divided the house into two equal parts. On either side of the partition the rafters and the tar-paper roof sloped down to low walls. The board walls were well battened down every crack. They were not finished inside; the bare studding stood against them. This was like Pa's house on the claim, but it was smaller and had no ceiling overhead.

The other room was very cold, of course. It had one window looking out at empty prairie covered with snow. Against the wall under the window was the sofa, a boughten sofa with a curved wooden back and one end curved up. A bed was made up, on the sofa. Brown calico curtains hung against the wall at each end of it, on a string that ran across above the window, so they could be pulled together and hide the sofa. Opposite it, a bed stood against the wall, and at the foot of the bed there was just space enough for a bureau and a trunk.

Laura hung her coat and muffler and veil and hood on nails behind the calico curtain, and set Ma's satchel on the floor under them. She stood shivering in the cold, not wanting to go into the warm room where Mrs Brewster was. But she had to, so she did.

Mr Brewster sat by the stove, holding the little boy on his knee. Mrs Brewster was scraping the gravy into a bowl. The table was set, with plates and knives carelessly askew on a smudged white cloth; the cloth was crooked on the table.

'May I help you, Mrs Brewster?' Laura said bravely. Mrs Brewster did not answer. She dumped potatoes angrily into a dish and thumped it on the table. The clock on the wall whirred, getting ready to strike, and Laura saw that the time was five minutes to four.

'Nowadays breakfast is so late, we eat only two meals a day,' Mr Brewster explained.

'Whose fault is it, I'd like to know!' Mrs Brewster blazed out. 'As if I didn't do enough, slaving from morning to night in this . . .'

Mr Brewster raised his voice. 'I only meant the days are so short . . .'

'Then say what you mean!' Mrs Brewster slammed the high chair to the table, snatched the little boy, and sat him in it, hard.

'Dinner's ready,' Mr Brewster said to Laura. She sat down in the vacant place. Mr Brewster passed her the potatoes and salt pork and gravy. The food was good but Mrs Brewster's silence was so unpleasant that Laura could hardly swallow.

'Is the schoolhouse far from here?' she tried to ask cheerfully.

Mr Brewster said, 'Half a mile, cross-lots. It's a claim shanty. The fellow that homesteaded that quarter section couldn't stick it out; he gave up and went back East.'

Then he, too, was silent. The little boy fretted, trying to reach everything on the table. Suddenly he flung his tin plate of food on the floor. Mrs Brewster slapped his hands, and he screamed. He went on screaming and kicking the table leg.

At last the meal was over. Mr Brewster took the milk pail from its nail on the wall and went to the stable. Mrs Brewster sat the little boy on the floor and gradually he stopped crying, while Laura helped to clear the table. Then she got an apron from Ma's satchel, tied it over her brown princess dress, and took a towel, to dry the dishes while Mrs Brewster washed them.

'What's your little boy's name, Mrs Brewster?' she asked. She hoped that Mrs Brewster would be more pleasant now.

'John,' said Mrs Brewster.

'That's such a nice name,' Laura said. 'People can call him Johnny while he's little, and then when he grows up, John is a good name for a man. Do you call him Johnny now?'

Mrs Brewster did not answer. The silence grew more and more dreadful. Laura felt her face grow burning hot. She went on wiping the dishes blindly. When they were done, Mrs Brewster threw out the dishwater and hung the pan on its nail. She sat in the rocking chair and rocked idly, while Johnny crawled under the stove and dragged the cat out by its tail. The cat scratched him and he bawled. Mrs Brewster went on rocking.

Laura did not dare to interfere. Johnny screamed, Mrs

Brewster sullenly rocked, and Laura sat in the straight chair by the table and looked out at the prairie. The road went straight across the snow and far away, out of sight. Twelve miles away was home. Ma was getting supper now; Carrie was home from school; they were laughing and talking with Grace. Pa would come in, and swing Grace up in his arms as he used to lift Laura when she was little. They would all go on talking at the supper table. Later they would sit in the lamplight, cosily reading while Carrie studied; then Pa would play the fiddle.

The room grew dark, and darker. Laura could not see the road any more. At last Mr Brewster came in with the milk. Then Mrs Brewster lighted the lamp. She strained the milk and set the pan away, while Mr Brewster sat down and opened a newspaper. Neither of them spoke. The unpleasant silence settled heavily down.

Laura did not know what to do; it was too early to go to bed. There was no other paper, and not a book in the room. Then she thought of her schoolbooks. Going into the cold, dark bedroom she groped in Ma's satchel and found her history book by the sense of touch. Taking it into the kitchen she sat down by the table again and began to study.

'At least, nothing hinders my studying,' she thought grimly. She felt hurt and sore as if she had been beaten, but gradually she forgot where she was, by keeping her mind fixed on history. At last she heard the clock strike eight. Then she stood up and said good night politely. Mrs Brewster did not answer, but Mr Brewster said, 'Good night.'

In the bedroom Laura shivered out of her dress and petticoats, and into her flannel nightgown. She got under the covers on the sofa and pulled the calico curtains around it. The pillow was of feathers, and there were sheets, and plenty of quilts, but the sofa was very narrow.

She heard Mrs Brewster talking angrily and very fast. The quilts were over Laura's head, so that only the tip of her nose was out in the cold, but she could not help hearing Mrs Brewster's quarrelling: '. . . suits you, but I keep a boarder!' she heard, and '. . . this horrible country out here! Schoolteacher, indeed! . . . been a teacher myself, if I hadn't married a . . .'

Laura thought: 'She doesn't want to board the teacher, that is all. She'd be as cross to anybody else.' She did her best not to hear any more, and to go to sleep. But all night, in her sleep, she was careful not to fall off the narrow sofa, and she was dreading tomorrow when she must begin to teach school.

2

First Day of School

Laura heard a stove lid rattle. For one instant she was in bed with Mary, and Pa was building the morning fire. Then she saw the calico curtain and she knew where she was, and that today she must begin to teach school.

She heard Mr Brewster take down the milk pail, and the door slammed behind him. On the other side of the curtain Mrs Brewster got out of bed. Johnny whimpered, and was still. Laura did not move; she felt that if she lay still enough, she might keep the day from coming.

Mr Brewster came in with the milk, and she heard him say, 'I'm going to start a fire in the schoolhouse. I'll be back by the time breakfast's ready.' The door slammed behind him again.

All at once, Laura threw back the covers. The air was biting cold. Her teeth chattered and her fingers were so stiff that she could not button her shoes.

The kitchen was not so cold. Mrs Brewster had broken the ice in the water pail and was filling the tea kettle, and she replied pleasantly to Laura's 'Good morning'. Laura filled the wash basin and washed her hands and face at the

11

bench by the door. The icy water made her cheeks tingle, and her whole face was rosy and glowing in the looking glass above the bench while she combed her hair before it.

Slices of salt pork were frying, and Mrs Brewster was slicing cold boiled potatoes into another frying pan on the stove. Johnny fussed in the bedroom, and Laura quickly pinned her braids, tied on her apron, and said, 'Let me fix the potatoes while you dress him.'

So while Mrs Brewster brought Johnny to the stove and made him ready for breakfast, Laura finished slicing the potatoes, and salted and peppered and covered them. Then she turned the slices of meat and set the table neatly.

'I'm glad Ma told me to bring this big apron,' she said. 'I like a real big apron that covers your whole dress, don't you?'

Mrs Brewster did not answer. The stove was red now and the whole room was warm, but it seemed bleak. Nothing but short, necessary words were said at the breakfast table.

It was a relief to Laura to put on her wraps, take her books and her tin dinner pail, and leave that house. She set out on the half-mile walk through the snow to the schoolhouse. The way was unbroken, except for Mr Brewster's footsteps, which were so far apart that Laura could not walk in them.

As she floundered on, plunging into the deep snow, she suddenly laughed aloud. 'Well!' she thought. 'Here I am, I dread to go on, and I would not go back. Teaching school can not possibly be as bad as staying in that house with Mrs Brewster. Anyway, it cannot be worse.'

Then she was so frightened that she said aloud, 'I've *got* to go on.' Black soft-coal smoke rose against the morning sky from the old claim shanty's stovepipe. Two more lines of footprints came to its door, and Laura heard voices inside it. For a moment she gathered her courage, then she opened the door and went in.

The board walls were not battened. Streaks of sunshine streamed through the cracks upon a row of six home-made seats and desks that marched down the middle of the room. Beyond them, on the studding of the opposite wall, a square of boards had been nailed and painted black, to make a blackboard.

In front of the seats stood a big heating stove. Its round sides and top were cherry-red from the heat of the fire, and standing around it were the scholars that Laura must teach. They all looked at Laura. There were five of them, and two boys and one girl were taller than she was.

'Good morning,' she managed to say.

They all answered, still looking at her. A small window by the door let in a block of sunshine. Beyond it, in the corner by the stove, stood a small table and a chair. 'That is the teacher's table,' Laura thought, and then, 'oh my; I am the teacher.'

Her steps sounded loud. All the eyes followed her. She

put her books and dinner pail on the table, and took off her coat and hood. She hung them on a nail in the wall by the chair. On the table was a small clock; its hands stood at five minutes to nine.

Somehow she had to get through five minutes, before the time to begin school.

Slowly she took off her mittens and put them in the pocket of her coat. Then she faced all the eyes, and stepped to the stove. She held her hands to it as if to warm them. All the pupils made way for her, still looking at her. She must say something. She must.

'It is cold this morning, isn't it?' she heard herself say; then without waiting for an answer, 'Do you think you can keep warm in the seats away from the stove?'

One of the tall boys said quickly, 'I'll sit in the back seat; it's the coldest.'

The tall girl said, 'Charles and I have to sit together, we have to study from the same books.'

'That's good; then you can all sit nearer the stove,' Laura said. To her joyful surprise, the five minutes were gone! She said, 'You may take your seats. School will begin.'

The little girl took the front seat; behind her sat the little boy, then the tall girl and Charles, and behind them the other tall boy. Laura rapped her pencil on the table. 'School will come to order. I will now take your names and ages.'

14

The little girl was Ruby Brewster; she was nine years old. She had brown hair and sparkling brown eyes, and she was as soft and still as a mouse. Laura knew she would be sweet and good. She had finished the First Reader, and in arithmetic she was learning subtraction.

The little boy was her brother Tommy Brewster. He was eleven, and had finished the Second Reader, and reached short-division.

The two sitting together were Charles and Martha Harrison. Charles was seventeen; he was thin and pale and slow of speech. Martha was sixteen; she was quicker, and spoke for them both.

The last boy was Clarence Brewster. He, too, was older than Laura. His brown eyes were even brighter and livelier than his little sister Ruby's, his dark hair was thick and unruly, and he was quick in speaking and moving. He had a way of speaking that was almost saucy.

Clarence, Charles, and Martha were all in the Fourth Reader. They had passed the middle of the spelling book, and in arithmetic they were working fractions. In geography they had studied the New England states, and they answered questions so well that Laura set them to learn the Middle Atlantic states. None of them had studied grammar or history, but Martha had brought her mother's grammar and Clarence had a history book.

'Very well,' Laura said. 'You may all begin at the beginning in grammar and history, and exchange the books, to learn your lessons.'

When Laura had learned all this, and assigned their lessons, it was time for recess. They all put on their wraps and went out to play in the snow, and Laura breathed a sigh of relief. The first quarter of the day was over.

Then she began to plan; she would have reading, arithmetic, and grammar lessons in the forenoon, and, in the afternoon, reading again, history, writing, and spelling. There were three classes in spelling, for Ruby and Tommy were far apart in the spelling book.

After fifteen minutes, she rapped on the window to call the pupils in. Then until noon she heard and patiently corrected their reading aloud.

The noon hour dragged slowly. Alone at her table, Laura ate her bread and butter, while the others gathered around the stove, talking and joking while they ate from their dinner pails. Then the boys ran races in the snow outdoors, while Martha and Ruby watched them from the window and Laura still sat at her table. She was a teacher now, and must act like one.

At last the hour was gone, and again she rapped on the window. The boys came briskly in, breathing out clouds of frosty breath and shaking cold air from their coats and mufflers as they hung them up. They were glowing from cold and exercise.

Laura said, 'The fire is low. Would you put more coal on, please, Charles?'

Willing, but slowly, Charles lifted the heavy hod of coal and dumped most of it into the stove.

'I'll do that next time!' Clarence said. Perhaps he did not mean to be impertinent. If he did mean to be, what could Laura do? He was a tough, hardy boy, bigger than she was, and older. His brown eyes twinkled at her. She stood as tall as possible and rapped her pencil on the table.

'School will come to order,' she said.

Though the school was small, she thought best to follow the routine of the town school, and have each class come forward to answer. Ruby was alone in her class, so she must know every answer perfectly, for there was no one to help her by answering some of the questions. Laura let her spell slowly, and if she made a mistake, she might try again. She spelled every word in her lesson. Tommy was slower, but Laura gave him time to think and try, and he did as well.

Then Martha and Charles and Clarence did their spelling. Martha made no mistakes, but Charles missed five words and Clarence missed three. For the first time, Laura must punish them.

'You may take your seat, Martha,' she said. 'Charles and Clarence, go to the blackboard, and write the words you missed, three times each.'

Charles slowly went, and began to write his words. Clarence glanced back at Laura with a saucy look. Rapidly he wrote large and scrawling letters that covered his half of the blackboard with only six words. Then turning towards Laura, and not even raising his hand for permission to speak, he said, 'Teacher! The board's too small.'

He was making a joke of punishment for failing in his lesson. He was defying Laura.

For a long, dreadful moment he stood laughing at her, and she looked straight at him.

Then she said, 'Yes, the board is small, Clarence. I am sorry, but you should erase what you have written and

18

write the words again more carefully. Make them smaller, and there will be room enough.'

He had to obey her, for she did not know what she could do if he did not.

Still grinning, good-naturedly he turned to the blackboard and wiped out the scrawls. He wrote the three words three times each, and below them he signed his name with a flourish.

With relief, Laura saw that it was four o'clock.

'You may put away your books,' she said. When every book was neat on the shelves beneath the desk tops, she said, 'School is dismissed.'

Clarence grabbed his coat and cap and muffler from their nail and with a shout he was first through the doorway. Tommy was at his heels, but they waited outside while Laura helped Ruby into her coat and tied her hood. More soberly, Charles and Martha wrapped themselves well against the cold before they set out. They had a mile to walk.

Laura stood by the window and watched them go. She could see Mr Brewster's brother's claim shanty, only half a mile away. Smoke blew from its stovepipe and its west window glinted back the light from the sinking sun. Clarence and Tommy scuffled in the snow, and Ruby's red hood bobbed along behind them. So far as Laura could see from the eastern window, the sky was clear.

The school shanty had no window from which she

could see the northwest. If a blizzard came up, she could not know that it was coming until it struck.

She cleaned the blackboard, and with the broom she swept the floor. A dustpan was not needed, the cracks between the floorboards were so wide. She shut the stove's draughts, put on her wraps, took her books and dinner pail, and shutting the door carefully behind her, she set out on her morning path towards Mrs Brewster's house.

Her first day as a teacher was over. She was thankful for that.

3

One Week

As she went trudging through the snow, Laura made herself feel cheerful. Mrs Brewster was hard to get acquainted with, Laura thought, but she could not always be cross. Perhaps this evening would not be unpleasant.

So Laura went in, snowy and glowing from the cold, and spoke cheerfully to Mrs Brewster. But to all her efforts, Mrs Brewster answered shortly or not at all. At supper, no one said a word. The stillness was so sullen and hateful that Laura could not speak.

After supper she helped with the work again, and sat again in the darkening room while Mrs Brewster silently rocked. She felt sick from wanting to be at home.

As soon as Mrs Brewster lighted the lamp, Laura brought her schoolbooks to the table. She set herself lessons, and determined to learn them before bedtime. She wanted to keep up with her class in town, and she hoped she could study hard enough to forget where she was.

She sat small in her chair, for the silence seemed to press against her from all sides. Mrs Brewster sat idle. Mr Brewster held Johnny asleep on his lap, and stared into the

21

fire through the stove's open draught. The clock struck seven. It struck eight. It struck nine. Then Laura made an effort, and spoke.

'It is getting late, and I'll say good night.'

Mrs Brewster paid no attention. Mr Brewster started, and said, 'Good night.'

Before Laura could hurry into bed in the cold dark, Mrs Brewster began to quarrel at him. Laura tried not to hear. She pulled the quilts over her head and pressed her ear tight against the pillow, but she could not help hearing. She knew then that Mrs Brewster wanted her to hear.

For Mrs Brewster said she'd not slave for a hoity-toity snip that had nothing to do but dress up and sit in a schoolhouse all day; she said that if Mr Brewster did not put Laura out of the house, she'd go back East without him. She went on and on, and the sound of her voice made Laura feel sick; it was a sound that enjoyed hurting people.

Laura did not know what to do. She wanted to go home, but she must not even think of home or she might cry. She must think what to do. There was nowhere else to stay; the other two houses in the settlement were only claim shanties. At the Harrisons', there were four in the one room, and at Mr Brewster's brother's house there were five. They could not possibly make room for Laura.

She did not really make Mrs Brewster any work, she

thought. She made her bed and helped with the kitchen work. Mrs Brewster was quarrelling now about the flat country and the wind and the cold; she wanted to go back East. Suddenly Laura understood; 'She isn't mad at *me*, she's only quarrelling about me because she wants to quarrel. She's a selfish, mean woman.'

Mr Brewster did not say a word. Laura thought: 'I've just got to bear it, too. There isn't anywhere else I can stay.'

When she woke in the morning she thought: 'I have only to get through one day at a time.'

It was hard to stay where she was not wanted. She took care to make no work for Mrs Brewster, and to help her all she could. Politely she said, 'Good morning,' and smiled, but she could not keep on smiling. She had not known before that it takes two to make a smile.

She dreaded the second school day, but it passed smoothly. Clarence idled instead of studying, and Laura dreaded that she must punish him again, but he knew his lessons. Perhaps she would have no trouble with him.

It was strange that she was so tired at four o'clock. The second day was over, and the first week would be half gone at noon tomorrow.

Suddenly Laura caught her breath, and stood stock-still on the snowy path. She had thought of Saturday and Sunday; two whole days in that house with Mrs Brewster. She heard herself say aloud, 'Oh, Pa. I can't.'

It was whimpering; she was ashamed when she heard it. No one else had heard. All around her the prairie was empty, white and far and still. She would rather stay there in the clean cold than go into the mean house or go back tomorrow to the anxious school day. But the sun was setting, and tomorrow it would rise; everything must go on.

That night Laura dreamed again that she was lost in a blizzard. She knew the dream; she had dreamed it sometimes, ever since she really had been lost with Carrie in a blizzard. But this blizzard was worse than before; now the stinging snow and the wind's hard blows tried to drive her and Carrie off the narrow sofa. Laura held on to Carrie with all her might for a long time, but suddenly Carrie was not there; the blizzard had got her. Laura's heart stopped in horror. She could not go on, she had no more strength; she sank down, down, into the dark. Then Pa came driving from town on the bobsled; he called to Laura, 'How about going home for Saturday, Half-Pint?' Ma and Mary and Carrie and Grace were so surprised! Mary said happily, 'Oh, Laura!' Ma's whole face lighted with her smiling. Carrie hurried to help Laura take off her wraps, and Grace jumped up and down, clapping her hands. 'Charles, why didn't you tell us!' Ma said, and Pa answered, 'Why, Caroline, I said I'd do a little hauling. Laura's little.' And Laura remembered how, at the dinner table, Pa had drunk his tea and pushed back his cup and said, 'Guess I'll do a little hauling this afternoon.' Ma said, 'Oh, Charles!' Laura had not gone away from home at all; she was there.

Then she woke up. She was at the Brewsters', and it was Wednesday morning. But the dream had been so real that she still almost believed it. Pa might come to take her home over Saturday. It was like him, to plan such a surprise.

There had been a snowstorm in the night. She had to break her path to the schoolhouse again. The early sunshine was faintly pink on miles of pure snow and every little shadow was thin blue. As Laura plunged and ploughed through the soft drifts, she saw Clarence breaking a path for Tommy and Ruby behind him. They floundered to the school shanty's door at the same time.

Little Ruby was covered from head to foot with snow, even her hood and her braids were snowy. Laura brushed her and told her to keep her wraps on until the room was warmer. Clarence put more coal on the fire while Laura shook her own wraps and swept the snow through the cracks between the floor boards. The sunshine streaming through the window made the shanty look warm, but it was colder than outdoors. But soon the good stove's warmth made their breath invisible; it was nine o'clock, and Laura said, 'School will come to order.'

Martha and Charles came in panting, three minutes late. Laura did not want to mark them tardy; they had to break their path, the whole mile. A few steps in deep snow are easy, and fun, but breaking a path is work that grows harder with every step. For a moment Laura thought of excusing Martha and Charles, this one time. But that would not be honest. No excuse could change the fact; they *were* tardy.

'I am sorry I must mark you tardy,' she said. 'But you may come to the stove and get warm before you take your seat.'

'We're sorry, Miss Ingalls,' Martha said. 'We didn't know it would take so long.'

'Breaking a path is hard work, I know,' said Laura, and suddenly she and Martha were smiling at each other, a friendly smile that made Laura feel as if teaching school were easy. She said, 'Second Reader class, rise. Pass to the front.' And Ruby, the Second Reader class, rose and came to stand before her.

The whole morning went smoothly. At noon, Ruby came to Laura's desk and shyly offered her a cookie. After dinners were eaten from the dinner pails, Clarence asked her to come out and snowball, and Martha said, 'Please do. Then we will have three on a side.'

Laura was so pleased to be asked, and so eager to be out in the sunshine and clean snow, that she went. It was great fun. She and Martha and Ruby fought against Charles, Clarence, and Tommy. The air was full of snowballs. Clarence and Laura were quickest of all, dodging and scooping and moulding the snow with their mittened hands and throwing and dodging again. Laura was glowing warm, and laughing, when a great burst of snow exploded in her eyes and her open mouth and plastered her whole face.

'Oh gee, I didn't mean to,' she heard Clarence saying.

'Yes, you did! It was a fair hit,' Laura answered, blindly rubbing her eyes.

'Here, let me; stand still,' he said. He took hold of her shoulder as if she were Ruby, and wiped her face with the end of her muffler.

'Thank you,' Laura said. But she knew that she must not play any more. She was too small and too young; she would not be able to keep her pupils in order if she played games with them.

That very afternoon Clarence pulled Martha's hair. Her brown braid whisked across his desk as she turned her head, and he caught it and gave it a tug.

'Clarence,' Laura said. 'Do not disturb Martha. Give your attention to your lessons.'

He gave her a friendly grin that said as plainly as words, 'All right, if you say so; I don't have to.'

To her horror, Laura almost smiled. Barely in time, she kept her look stern. Now she was sure that she would have trouble with Clarence.

Wednesday was gone. There were only Thursday and Friday. Laura tried not to expect that Pa would come for her, but she could not stop hoping. It would be so like Pa to come and save her from a miserable two days in Mrs Brewster's house. But of course he did not know how miserable it was. She must not expect him. But surely he might come, if the weather were good. If he came, there were only two more evenings to endure, and then – Friday night at home! Still she did not expect him; she must not, or she would be so disappointed if he did not come. They were missing her at home, she knew; if the weather were pleasant, surely he would come.

But Friday morning the sky was stormy and the wind was colder.

All day at school Laura listened to the wind, afraid that its sound would change to a blizzard's howl and the shanty suddenly shake and the window go blank.

The wind blew colder through the cracks. Its sound rose, and from every drift the snow scudded across the prairie. Laura knew now that Pa would not come. Twenty-four miles in such weather was too much for the horses.

'How am I going to get through the time till Monday?' Laura thought.

Wretchedly she turned her eyes from the window, and saw Charles sitting half-asleep. Suddenly he jumped, wide awake. Clarence had jabbed his arm with a pin. Almost Laura laughed, but Clarence caught her glance and his eyes laughed. She could not let this pass.

'Clarence,' she said. 'Why aren't you studying?'

28

'I know all my lessons,' he replied.

She did not doubt it. Clarence learned quickly; he could keep up with Martha and Charles and have plenty of idle time.

'We will see how well you know your spelling,' she said. She tapped upon her table. 'Third spelling class, rise. Come forward.'

The shanty trembled in the wind that every moment howled louder around it. Heat from the red-cheeked stove melted the snow that was blown through the cracks and made wet streaks on the floor. Clarence correctly spelled every word that Laura gave him, while she wondered whether she should dismiss school early. If she waited and the storm grew worse, Charles and Martha might never reach their home.

It seemed to her that the wind had a strangely silvery sound. She listened; they all listened. She did not know what to make of it. The sky was not changed; grey, low clouds were moving fast above the prairie covered with blowing snow. The strange sound grew clearer, almost like music. Suddenly the whole air filled with a chiming of little bells. Sleigh bells!

Everyone breathed again, and smiled. Two brown horses swiftly passed the window. Laura knew them; they were Prince and Lady, young Mr Wilder's horses! The sleigh bells rang louder, and stopped; then a few bells shook out small tinkles. The brown horses were standing close outside the south wall, in the shelter of the shanty.

Laura was so excited that she had to steady her voice. 'The class may be seated.' She waited a moment; then, 'You may all put away your books. It is a little early, but the storm is growing worse. School is dismissed.'

4

Sleigh Bells

Clarence dashed outdoors, and back again, shouting, 'It's someone for you, Teacher!'

Laura was helping Ruby into her coat. 'Tell him I will be there in a minute.'

'Come on, Charles! You ought to see his horses!' Clarence slammed the door so that the shanty shook. Laura quickly put on her coat and tied her hood and muffler. She shut the stove's draughts, thrust her hands into her mittens, and took her books and dinner pail. She made sure the door was fastened behind her. All the time she was so excited that she could hardly breathe. Pa had not come, but she was going home, after all!

Almanzo Wilder was sitting in a cutter so low and small that it was hardly more than a heap of furs on the snow behind Prince and Lady. He was muffled in a buffalo coat and a fur cap with flaps that was as snug as a hood.

He did not step out into the storm. Instead, he lifted the fur robes and gave Laura his hand to help her step into the cutter. Then he tucked the robes around her. They were furry, warm buffalo skins, lined with flannel.

31

'You want to stop at Brewster's?' he asked.

'I must, to leave the dinner pail and get my satchel,' Laura said.

In the Brewster house Johnny was screaming angrily, and when Laura came out of the house she saw Almanzo looking at it with disgust. But it was all behind her now; she was going home. Almanzo tucked the robes snugly around her, the sleigh bells began merrily ringing, and swiftly behind the brown horses she was going home.

She said through her thick black woollen veil, 'It's nice of you to come for me. I was hoping Pa would come.'

Almanzo hesitated. 'We . . . ell. He was figuring he would, but I told him it's a drive that would be pretty hard on his team.'

'They'll have to bring me back,' Laura said doubtfully. 'I must be at school Monday morning.'

'Maybe Prince and Lady could make the drive again,' Almanzo said.

Laura was embarrassed; she had not meant to hint. She had not even thought of his bringing her back. Again, she had spoken before she thought. How right Pa's advice had been; she should always, always, think before she spoke. She thought: 'After this, I shall always think before I speak,' and she said, without thinking how rude it would sound, 'Oh, you needn't bother. Pa will bring me back.'

'It would be no bother,' Almanzo said. 'I told you I'd take you for a sleigh ride when I got my cutter made.

This is the cutter. How do you like it?'

'I think it's fun to ride in; it's so little,' Laura answered.

'I made it smaller than the boughten ones. It's only five feet long, and twenty-six inches wide at the bottom. Makes it snugger to ride in, and lighter for the horses to pull,' Almanzo explained. 'They hardly know they're pulling anything.'

'It's like flying!' Laura said. She had never imagined such wonderful speed.

The low clouds raced backward overhead, the blown snow smoked backward on either side, and swiftly onward went the glossy brown horses, streaming music from their strings of bells. There was not a jolt nor a jar; the little cutter skimmed the snow as smoothly as a bird in air.

Almost too soon, though not soon enough, they were flashing past the windows of Main Street, and here was Pa's front door again, opening, and Pa standing in it. Laura was out of the cutter and up the steps before she thought; then, 'Oh, thank you, Mr Wilder; good night!' she called back all in a breath, and she was at home.

Ma's smile lighted her whole face. Carrie came running to unwind Laura's muffler and veil, while Grace clapped her hands and shouted, 'Laura's come home!' Then Pa came in and said, 'Let's look at you. Well, well, the same little flutter-budget!'

There was so much to say and to tell. The big sitting room had never looked so beautiful. The walls were dark brown now; every year the pine boards grew darker. The table was covered with the red-checked cloth, and the braided rag rugs were gay on the floor. The rocking chairs stood by the white-curtained windows; Mary's boughten chair, and the willow chair that Pa had made for Ma so long ago in the Indian territory. The patchwork cushions were in them, and there was Ma's work-basket and her knitting with the needles thrust into the ball of yarn. Kitty lazily stretched and yawned, and came to curve purring against Laura's ankles. There on Pa's desk was the blue-bead basket that Mary had made.

The talking went on at the supper table; Laura was more hungry for talk than food. She told about each one of her pupils at school, and Ma told of Mary's latest letter;

Mary was doing so well in the college for the blind, in Iowa. Carrie told all the news of the school in town. Grace told of the words she had learned to read, and of Kitty's last fight with a dog.

After supper, when Laura and Carrie had done the dishes, Pa said as Laura had been hoping he would, 'If you'll bring me the fiddle, Laura, we'll have a little music.'

He played the brave marching songs of Scotland and of the United States; he played the sweet old love songs and the gay dance tunes, and Laura was so happy that her throat ached.

When it was bedtime and she went upstairs with Carrie and Grace, she looked from the attic window at the lights of the town twinkling here and there, through the wind and the blowing snow. As she snuggled under the quilts she heard Pa and Ma coming up to their room at the head of the stairs. She heard Ma's pleasant low voice and Pa's deeper one answering it, and she was so glad to be at home for two nights and nearly two days that she could hardly go to sleep.

Even her sleep was deep and good, without fear of falling off a narrow sofa. Almost at once, it seemed her eyes opened; she heard the stove lid rattle downstairs, and knew that she was at home.

'Good morning!' Carrie said from her bed, and Grace bounced up and cried, 'Good morning, Laura!' 'Good morning,' Ma smiled when Laura entered the kitchen, and Pa came in with the milk and said, 'Good morning, flutterbudget!' Laura had never noticed before that saying, 'Good morning,' made the morning good. Anyway, she was learning something from that Mrs Brewster, she thought.

Breakfast was so pleasant. Then briskly, and still talking, Laura and Carrie did the dishes, and went upstairs to make the beds. While they were tucking in a sheet, Laura said, 'Carrie, do you ever think how lucky we are to have a home like this?'

Carrie looked around her, surprised. There was nothing to be seen but the two beds, the three boxes under the eaves where they kept their things, and the underside of the shingles overhead. There was also the stovepipe that came up through the floor and went out through the roof.

'It *is* snug,' Carrie said, while they spread the first quilt and folded and tucked in its corners. 'I guess I never did think, exactly.'

'You wait till you go away,' Laura said. 'Then you'll think.'

'Do you dreadfully hate to teach school?' Carrie asked her, low.

'Yes, I do,' Laura almost whispered. 'But Pa and Ma mustn't know.'

They plumped up the pillows and set them in their places, and went to Laura's bed. 'Maybe you won't have to, long,' Carrie consoled her. They unbuttoned the straw tick and thrust their arms deep into it, stirring up the straw. 'Maybe you'll get married. Ma did.'

'I don't want to,' Laura said. She patted the tick smooth and buttoned it. 'There. Now the bottom quilt. I'd rather stay home than anything.'

'Always?' Carrie asked.

'Yes, always,' Laura said, and she meant it with all her heart. She spread the sheet. 'But I can't, not all the time. I have to go on teaching school.'

They tucked in the quilts and plumped up Laura's pillow. The beds were done. Carrie said she would do the sweeping. 'I always do, now,' she said, 'and if you're going to Mary Power's, the sooner you go the sooner you'll be back.'

'I only have to find out if I'm keeping up with my class,' Laura said. Downstairs, she set the wash-boiler on the stove and filled it with pails of water from the well. Then while it was heating, she went to see Mary Power.

She had quite forgotten that she had ever disliked the town. It was bright and brisk this morning. Sunlight glinted on the icy ruts of snow in the street and sparkled on the frosty edges of the board sidewalk. In the two blocks there were only two vacant lots on the west side of the street now, and some of the stores were painted, white or grey. Harthorne's grocery was painted red. Everywhere there was the stir and bustle of morning. The storekeepers in thick coats and caps were scraping trodden bits of snow from the sidewalk before their stores, and talking and joking as they worked. Doors slammed; hens cackled, and horses whinnied in the stables.

Mr Fuller, and then Mr Bradley, lifted their caps and said good morning to Laura as she passed. Mr Bradley said, 'I hear you're teaching Brewster school, Miss Ingalls.'

Laura felt very grown-up. 'Yes,' she said, 'I am in town only over Saturday.'

'Well, I wish you all success,' said Mr Bradley.

'Thank you, Mr Bradley,' said Laura.

In Mr Power's tailor shop, Mary's father sat cross-legged on his table, sewing busily. Mary was helping her mother with the morning's work in the back room.

'Well, look who's here!' Mrs Power exclaimed. 'How's the schoolteacher?'

'Very well, thank you,' Laura replied.

'Do you like teaching school?' Mary wanted to know.

'I'm getting along all right, I guess,' Laura said. 'But I'd rather be home. I'll be glad when the two months are over.'

'So will all of us,' Mary told her. 'My, we do miss you at school.'

Laura was pleased. 'Do you?' she said. 'I miss you, too.'

'Nellie Oleson tried to get your seat,' Mary went on. 'But Ida wouldn't let her. Ida said she's keeping that seat for you till you come back, and Mr Owen said she can.'

'Whatever did Nellie Oleson want my seat for?' Laura exclaimed. 'Her's is just as good, or almost.'

'That's Nellie for you,' said Mary. 'She just wants anything that anybody else has, that's all. Oh Laura, she'll be fit to be tied when I tell her that Almanzo Wilder brought you home in his new cutter!'

They both laughed. Laura felt a little ashamed, but she could not help laughing. They remembered Nellie's bragging that she was going to ride behind those brown horses. And she never had done it yet.

'I can hardly wait,' Mary said.

Mrs Power said, 'I don't think that's very nice, Mary.'

'I know it isn't,' Mary admitted. 'But if you only knew how that Nellie Oleson's always bragging and showing off, and picking on Laura. And now to think that Laura's teaching school, and Almanzo Wilder's beauing her home.'

'Oh, no! He isn't!' Laura cried out. 'It isn't like that at all. He came for me as a favour to Pa.'

Mary laughed. 'He must think a lot of your Pa!' she began to tease; then she looked at Laura and said, 'I'm sorry. I won't talk about it if you don't want to.'

'I don't mean that,' Laura said. Everything is simple when you are alone, or at home, but as soon as you meet other people you are in difficulties. 'I just don't want you to think Mr Wilder's my beau, because he isn't.'

'All right,' Mary said.

'And I only ran in for a minute,' Laura explained. 'I put wash-water on, and it must be hot now. Tell me where you are in your lessons, Mary.'

When Mary told her, Laura saw that she was keeping up with the class by her studying at night. Then she went home.

All that day was such a happy time. Laura did her washing and sprinkled and ironed the clean, fresh clothes. Then in the cosy sitting room she ripped her beautiful brown velvet hat, talking all the time with Ma and Carrie and Grace. She brushed and steamed the velvet and draped it again over the buckram frame, and tried it on. It looked like a new hat, even more becoming than before. There was just time enough to brush and sponge and press her brown dress, and then to help Ma get an early supper. Afterwards they all bathed one by one in the warm kitchen, and went to bed.

'If I could only live like this always, I'd never want anything more,' Laura thought as she went to sleep. 'But maybe I appreciate it more because I have only tonight and tomorrow morning . . .'

The morning sunshine and the sky had their quiet, Sunday look, and the town was quiet with a Sunday stillness when Laura and Carrie and Grace and Ma sedately went out on Sunday morning. The morning work was done, the beans for Sunday dinner were baking slowly in the oven. Pa carefully closed the heating-stove's draughts, and came out and locked the door.

Laura and Carrie went ahead; Pa and Ma came behind them, holding Grace's hands. All fresh and clean and dressed in Sunday best, they walked slowly in the cold Sunday morning, taking care not to slip on the icy paths. Carefully along the street and single file across lots behind Fuller's store, everyone else was going towards the church, too.

As she went in, Laura looked eagerly over the partly filled seats, and there was Ida! Ida's brown eyes danced when she saw Laura, and she slid along the seat to make room, and gave Laura's arm a squeeze. 'My, I'm glad to see you!' she whispered. 'When did you come?'

'Friday after school. I've got to go back this afternoon,' Laura answered. There was a little time to talk before Sunday School.

'Do you like teaching?' Ida asked.

'No, I do not! But don't tell anybody else. I'm getting along all right so far.'

'I won't,' Ida promised. 'I knew you would. But your place at school is awfully empty.'

'I'll be back. It's only seven weeks more,' Laura said.

'Laura,' Ida said. 'You don't care if Nellie Oleson sits with me while you're gone, do you?'

'Why, Ida Brow . . .' Laura began. Then she saw that Ida was only teasing. 'Of course not,' she said. 'You ask her and see if she will.'

Because they were in church and could not laugh, they sat silently shaking and almost choking in their effort to keep their faces sober. Lawyer Barnes was rapping the pulpit to bring the Sunday School to order, and they could not talk any more. They must rise and join in the singing.

> 'Sweet Sabbath School! more dear to me
> Than fairest palace dome,
> My heart e'er turns with joy to thee,
> My own dear Sabbath home.'

Singing together was even better than talking. Ida was such a dear, Laura thought, as they stood side by side holding the hymn book open before them.

> 'Here first my wilful, wandering heart
> The way of life was shown;
> Here first I sought the better part
> And gained a Sabbath home.'

Clear and sure, Laura's voice held the note while Ida's soft alto chimed, 'Sabbath home.' Then their voices blended again:

> 'My heart e'er turns with joy to thee,
> My own dear Sabbath home.'

Sunday School was the pleasant part of church. Though they could talk only to the teacher about the lesson, Ida and Laura could smile at each other and sing together.

When Sunday School ended, there was only time to say, 'Good-bye. Good-bye.' Then Ida must sit with Mrs Brown in the front seat while Reverend Brown preached one of his long, stupid sermons.

Laura and Carrie went to sit with Pa and Ma and Grace. Laura made sure that she remembered the text, to repeat at home when Pa asked her; then she need not listen any more. She always missed Mary in church. Mary had always sat so properly beside her, watchful that Laura behaved. It was strange to think that they had been little girls, and now Mary was in college and Laura was a schoolteacher. She tried not to think of Mrs Brewster's, and of school. After all, Mary had gone to college, and now Laura was earning forty dollars; with forty dollars, Mary could surely stay in college next year. Maybe everything comes out all right, if you keep on trying. Anyway, you have to keep on trying; nothing will come out right if you don't. 'If I can only manage Clarence for seven weeks more,' Laura thought.

Carrie pinched her arm. Everyone was standing up, to sing the Doxology. Church was over.

Dinner was so good. Ma's baked beans were delicious, and the bread and butter and little cucumber pickles, and everyone was so comfortable, so cheerful and talking. Laura said, 'Oh, I do like it here!'

'It's too bad that Brewster's isn't a better place to stay,' said Pa.

'Why, Pa, I haven't complained,' Laura said in surprise.

'I know you haven't,' said Pa. 'Well, keep a stiff upper lip; seven weeks will soon be gone, and you'll be home again.'

How pleasant it was, after the dishes were done, when they were all settled in the front room for Sunday afternoon. Sunshine streamed through the clean windows into the warm room, where Ma sat gently rocking, and Carrie and Grace pored over the pictures in Pa's big green book, *The Wonders of the Animal World*. Pa read items from the *Pioneer Press* to Ma, and at his desk Laura sat writing a letter to Mary. Carefully with Ma's little pearl-handled pen that was shaped like a feather, she wrote of her school and her pupils. Of course she wrote of nothing unpleasant. The clock ticked, and now and then Kitty lazily stretched and purred a short purr.

When the letter was finished, Laura went upstairs and packed her clean clothes in Ma's satchel. She brought it downstairs and into the front room. It must be time to go, but Pa sat reading his paper and took no notice.

Ma looked at the clock and said gently, 'Charles, surely you must hitch up, or you'll be late starting. It's a long way to go and come, and dark comes early nowadays.'

Pa only turned a page of the paper and said, 'Oh, there's no hurry.'

Laura and Ma looked at each other in amazement. They looked at the clock, and again at Pa. He did not stir, but his brown beard had a smiling look. Laura sat down.

The clock ticked, and Pa silently read the paper. Twice Ma almost spoke, and changed her mind. At last, not looking up, Pa said, 'Some folks worry about my team.'

'Why, Charles! There isn't anything wrong with the horses?' Ma exclaimed.

'Well,' said Pa. 'They're not as young as they used to be, for a fact. They can still hold out pretty well, though, for twelve miles and back.'

'Charles,' Ma said helplessly.

Pa looked up at Laura and his eyes were twinkling. 'Maybe I don't have to drive 'em so far,' he said. Sleigh bells were coming down the street. Clearer and louder they came; then rang all at once and stopped by the door. Pa went to the door and opened it.

'Good afternoon, Mr Ingalls,' Laura heard Almanzo Wilder say. 'I stopped by to see if Laura would let me drive her out to her school.'

'Why, I'm sure she'd like a ride in that cutter,' Pa replied.

'It's getting late, and too cold to tie 'em without blanketing,' Almanzo said. 'I'll drive down the street and stop on my way back.'

'I'll tell her,' Pa answered, and shut the door while the bells jingled away. 'How about it, Laura?'

'It is fun to ride in a cutter,' Laura said. Quickly she tied on her hood and got into her coat. The bells were coming; she had hardly time to say good-bye before they stopped at the door.

'Don't forget the satchel,' Ma said, and Laura turned back to snatch it up.

'Thank you, Ma. Good-bye,' she said and went out to the cutter. Almanzo helped her in and tucked the robes around her. Prince and Lady started quickly; all the bells rang out their music, and she was on her way back to her school.

5

A Stiff Upper Lip

All that week, everything went wrong; everything. Nothing gave Laura the least encouragement.

The weather was sullen. Dull clouds lay low and flat above the grey-white prairie, and the wind blew monotonously. The cold was damp and clammy. The stoves smoked.

Mrs Brewster let the housework go. She did not sweep out the snow that Mr Brewster tracked in; it melted and made puddles with the ashes around the stove. She did not make their bed nor even spread it up. Twice a day she cooked potatoes and salt pork and put them on the table. The rest of the time she sat brooding. She did not even comb her hair, and it seemed to Laura that Johnny squalled with temper that whole week.

Once Laura tried to play with him, but he only struck at her and Mrs Brewster said angrily, 'Leave him alone!'

After supper he went to sleep on his father's knee, and Mr Brewster just sat. The air seemed to smoulder with Mrs Brewster's silence, and he sat, Laura thought, like a bump on a log. She had heard that said, but she had not realized what it meant. A bump on a log does not fight anyone, but it cannot be budged.

The silence was so loud that Laura could hardly study. When she went to bed, Mrs Brewster quarrelled at Mr Brewster. She wanted to go back East.

Laura could hardly have studied well, anyway; she was so worried about her school. In spite of all she could do, everything went from bad to worse.

It began on Monday, when Tommy did not know one word of his spelling lesson. Ruby would not let him have the speller, he said.

'Why, Ruby!' Laura said in surprise. Then sweet little Ruby turned into a very spitfire. Laura was so startled that before she could stop them, Ruby and Tommy were quarrelling.

Sternly Laura stopped that. She went to Tommy's seat and gave him the speller. 'Now learn that lesson,' said she. 'You may stay in at recess and recite it to me.'

Next day, Ruby did not know her lesson. She stood before Laura with her hands behind her, innocent as a kitten, and said, 'I could not learn it, Teacher. You gave Tommy the speller.'

Laura remembered to count ten. Then she said, 'So I did. Well, you and Tommy may sit together to learn your spelling.'

They were not studying the same lessons in the book, but they could hold it open in two places. Leaning to one side, Tommy could study his lesson while Ruby, leaning to the other side, could study hers. In that way, Laura and Mary used to learn their different lessons in Ma's speller.

But Tommy and Ruby did not. They sat silently struggling, each to open the book wider at his place. Again and again Laura said sharply, 'Tommy! Ruby!' But neither of them learned their spelling well.

Martha could not work her arithmetic problems. Charles sat idly staring at the window, where nothing was to be seen but the grey weather. When Laura told him to keep his eyes on his lessons, he stared day-dreaming at a page. Laura knew he was not seeing it.

She was too little. When Martha and Charles and Clarence stood before her to answer, they were too much for her. Though she did her best, she could not interest them in learning even geography and history.

On Monday, Clarence knew part of his history lesson, but when Laura asked him when the first settlement was made in Virginia, he answered carelessly, 'Oh, I didn't study that part.'

'Why didn't you?' Laura asked.

'The lesson was too long,' Clarence replied, with a look from narrow, laughing eyes that said, 'what are you going to do about that?'

Laura was furiously angry, but as her eyes met his she knew that he expected her to be angry. What could she do? She couldn't punish him; he was too big. She must not show any anger.

So she kept quiet, while she turned the pages of the history consideringly. Her heart was faint, but she must not let him know that. Finally she said, 'It is too bad that you did not learn this. It will make your next lesson so much longer, for we must not keep Charles and Martha back.'

She went on hearing Charles and Martha answer on the lesson. Then she gave them all another lesson of the usual length.

The next day Clarence did not know his history at all. 'It's no use trying to learn such long lessons,' he said.

'If you do not want to learn, Clarence, you are the

loser,' Laura told him. She kept on asking him questions in his turn, hoping that he would grow ashamed of answering, 'I don't know.' But he did not.

Every day she felt more miserably that she was failing. She could not teach school. Her first school would be a failure; she would not be able to get another certificate. She would earn no more money. Mary would have to leave college, and that would be Laura's fault. She could hardly learn her own lessons, though she studied them not only at night, but at noon recess. When she went back to town, she would be behind her class.

All the trouble came from Clarence. He could make Ruby and Tommy behave, if he would; he was their older brother. He could learn his lessons; he was much smarter than Martha and Charles. How she wished that she were big enough to give Clarence the whipping he deserved.

Slowly the week dragged by, the longest and most miserable week that Laura had ever known.

On Thursday, when Laura said, 'Third arithmetic class, rise,' Clarence stood up quickly and Charles began to move languidly, but Martha half rose and yelled, 'Ow!' and sat down as if she were jerked.

Clarence had driven his knife through her braid and pinned it to his desk. He had done it so quietly that Martha knew nothing of it until she tried to stand up.

'Clarence!' Laura said. He did not stop laughing. Tommy was laughing, Ruby was giggling, even Charles was grinning. Martha sat red-faced, with tears in her eyes.

Laura was in despair. They were all against her; she could not discipline them. Oh, how could they be so mean! For an instant she remembered Miss Wilder, who had failed to teach the school in town. 'This is the way she felt,' Laura thought.

Then suddenly she was very angry. She yanked the knife up, and clicked it shut in her fist. She did not feel small as she faced Clarence. 'Shame on you!' she said, and he stopped laughing. They were all still.

Laura marched back to her table, and rapped on it. 'Third class in arithmetic, rise! Come forward.'

They did not know the lesson; they could not solve the problems, but at least they went through the motions of trying. Laura felt tall and terrible, and they obeyed her meekly. At last she said, 'You may all repeat this lesson tomorrow. Class is dismissed.'

Her head ached as she went towards Mrs Brewster's hateful house. She could not be angry all the time, and discipline was no good if the pupils would not learn their lessons. Ruby and Tommy were far behind in spelling, Martha could not parse a simple compound sentence nor add fractions, and Clarence was learning no history. Laura tried to hope that she could do better tomorrow.

Friday was quiet. Everyone was dull and listless. They were only waiting for the week to end, and so was she. The hands of the clock had never moved so slowly.

In the afternoon the clouds began to break and the light grew brighter. Just before four o'clock, pale sunshine streamed eastward across the snowy land. Then Laura heard sleigh bells faintly ringing.

'You may put away your books,' she said. That miserable week was ended, at last. Nothing more could happen now. 'School is dismissed.'

The music of the bells came ringing louder and clearer. Laura's coat was buttoned and her hood tied when Prince and Lady passed the window with the dancing bells. She snatched up her books and dinner pail, and then the worst thing of all happened.

Clarence opened the door, thrust his head in, and shouted, 'Teacher's beau's here!'

Almanzo Wilder must have heard. He could not help hearing. Laura did not know how she could face him. What could she say? How could she tell him that she had given Clarence no reason to say such a thing?

He was waiting in the cold wind, and the horses were not blanketed; she must go out. It seemed to her that he was smiling, but she could hardly look at him. He tucked her in and said, 'All snug?'

'Yes, thank you,' she answered. The horses went swiftly, their strings of bells merrily ringing. It would be better to say nothing of Clarence, Laura decided; as Ma would say, 'Least said, soonest mended.'

6

Managing

While Pa played the fiddle that evening at home, Laura felt much better. Two weeks were gone, she thought; there were but six more. She could only keep on trying. The music stopped, and Pa asked, 'What's the trouble, Laura? Don't you want to make a clean breast of it?'

She had not meant to worry them; she intended to say nothing that was not cheerful. But suddenly she said, 'Oh, Pa, I don't know what to do!'

She told them all about that miserable week at school. 'What can I do?' she asked, 'I must do something; I *can't* fail. But I am failing. If only I were big enough to whip Clarence. That's what he needs, but I can't.'

'You might ask Mr Brewster to,' Carrie suggested. 'He could make Clarence behave himself.'

'Oh, but Carrie!' Laura protested. 'How can I tell the school board that I can't manage the school? No, I can't do that.'

'There you have it, Laura!' Pa said. 'It's all in that word, "manage". You might not get far with Clarence, even if you were big enough to punish him as he deserves. Brute force can't do much. Everybody's born free, you know, like it says in the Declaration of Independence. You can lead a horse to water, but you can't make him drink, and good or bad, nobody but Clarence can ever boss Clarence. You better just manage.'

'Yes, I know, Pa,' Laura said. 'But how?'

'Well, first of all, be patient. Try to see things his way, so far as you can. Better not try to make him do anything, because you can't. He doesn't sound to me like a really vicious boy.'

'No, he isn't,' Laura agreed. 'But I guess I just don't know how to manage him.'

'If I were you,' Ma gently began, and Laura remembered that Ma had been a schoolteacher, 'I'd give way to Clarence, and not pay any attention to him. It's attention he wants; that's why he plays up. Be pleasant and nice to him, but put all your attention on the others and straighten them out. Clarence'll come around.'

'That's right, Laura, listen to your Ma,' said Pa. '"Wise as a serpent and gentle as a dove."'

'Charles!' said Ma. Pa took up his fiddle and began saucily playing to her, 'Can she make a cherry pie, Billy boy, Billy boy; can she make a cherry pie, charming Billy?'

Sunday afternoon, when Laura was flying over the sunny snow in the cutter, Almanzo Wilder said, 'It chirks you up to go home over Sunday. I've got an idea it's pretty tough, staying at Brewster's.'

'It's my first school, and I never was away from home before,' Laura answered. 'I get homesick. I do appreciate your driving so far to take me home.'

'It's a pleasure,' he said.

It was polite of him to say so, but Laura saw no pleasure for him in that long, cold drive. They hardly said a word the whole way, because of the cold, and she knew very well that she would not be entertaining anyway. She could hardly ever think of anything to say to strangers.

The horses were so warm from trotting that they must not stand one moment in the cold wind, so at the Brewsters' door he stopped them only long enough for Laura to jump quickly out. As they went on, he touched his fur cap with his gloved hand and called through the sleigh bells' music, 'Good-bye till Friday!'

Laura felt guilty. She had not expected him to make that long drive every week. She hoped he did not think that she was expecting him to do it. Surely, he was not thinking of . . . well, of maybe being her beau?

She was almost used to Mrs Brewster's miserable house. She had only to forget it, as well as she could; to study until bedtime, and in the mornings to make her bed neatly, swallow her breakfast and wipe the dishes, and get away to school. There were only six weeks more, now.

On Monday morning, school began as glumly as it had

ended on Friday. But Laura was determined to make a change, and she began at once.

When Tommy had stumbled through his reading lesson she smiled at him and said, 'Your reading is improving, Tommy. You deserve a reward. Would you like to copy your spelling lesson on the blackboard?'

Tommy smiled, so she gave him the spelling book and a new piece of chalk. When he had copied his lesson, she praised his writing and told him that now he could study his spelling from the board. She gave the spelling book to Ruby.

'Your reading lesson was very good, too,' she said to Ruby. 'So tomorrow, would you like to copy your spelling lesson on the blackboard?'

'Oh, yes, ma'am!' Ruby answered eagerly, and Laura thought, 'There! that's one thing managed.'

Clarence fidgeted, dropped his books, and pulled Martha's hair, but Laura remembered Ma's advice and did not see him. Poor Martha did not know her grammar lesson at all; she was so hopelessly confused about complex and compound sentences that she had stopped trying to understand them. She answered only, 'I don't know. I don't know.'

'I think you must take this lesson over, Martha,' Laura had to say, and then she had an inspiration and went on, 'I would like to go over it again myself. I am trying to keep up with my class in town, and grammar is hard. If you would like to, we can go through this lesson together at the noon hour. Would you like to?'

'Yes, I would,' Martha answered.

So at noon, when they had eaten their dinners, Laura took up her grammar and said, 'Ready, Martha?' Martha smiled back at her.

Then Clarence asked, 'Is that why you study all the time, to keep up with your class in town?'

'Yes, I study at night but I have to study here, too,' Laura answered, passing by him towards the blackboard. Clarence whistled, 'Whew!' under his breath, but Laura paid no attention.

At the blackboard she worked with Martha until Martha could diagram a complex compound sentence all by herself. Martha said, 'I understand it now! After this, I won't dread the grammar questions so much.'

So that was the trouble, Laura thought. Martha had dreaded grammar so much that she could not learn it.

'Don't dread a lesson,' Laura said. 'I'll always be glad to study any of them with you, if you want me to.' Martha's brown eyes smiled almost like Ida's as she said, 'I would like to, sometimes. Thank you.' Laura wished that she need not be the teacher; she and Martha were the same age, and might have been friends.

She had decided what to do about Clarence's history lessons. He was far behind Charles and Martha, but Laura asked him no questions that he could not answer, and when she set the lesson for next day she said, 'This doesn't mean you, Clarence; it would make your lesson far too long. Let me see. How many pages are you behind?'

He showed her, and she said, 'How many do you think you can learn? Would three be too much?'

'No,' he said. There was nothing else he could say, no contention he could make.

'Then the class is dismissed,' Laura said. She wondered what Clarence would do. Pa's advice and Ma's was working well so far, but would it work with Clarence?

She did not ask him many questions next day, but he seemed to know the three pages perfectly. Charles and Martha were now nine pages ahead of him. Laura set them seven pages more, and said to Clarence, 'Would another three pages be too much? You may take that much if you like.'

'I'll learn it,' Clarence said, and this time he looked at Laura with a friendly smile.

She was so surprised that she almost smiled back. But she said quickly, 'Make it shorter if it is too much.'

'I'll learn it,' Clarence repeated.

'Very well,' Laura said. 'Class dismissed.'

She was becoming adjusted to the pattern of the days. A silent breakfast in the chill of early morning, a shivering walk to the cold school shanty; then the usual round of lessons, with recess and noon breaking it into four equal parts. Then the cold walk back to the Brewsters' house for a cheerless supper, an evening of study, and sleep on the narrow sofa. Mrs Brewster was always sullen and silent. She seldom even quarrelled at Mr Brewster any more.

The week passed and Friday came again. When the history class came forward to answer, Clarence said, 'You may hear me as far as Martha and Charles. I've caught up with them.'

Laura was amazed. She exclaimed, 'But how could you, Clarence?'

'If you can study at night, I can,' Clarence said. Laura almost smiled at him again. She could have liked him so much, if she had not been the teacher. The brown sparkles in his eyes were like the blue sparkles in Pa's. But she was the teacher.

'That is good,' she said. 'Now you can all three go on together.'

With four o'clock came the music of sleigh bells, and Clarence loudly whispered, 'Teacher's beau!'

Laura's cheeks grew hot, but she said quietly, 'You may put away your books. School is dismissed.'

She dreaded that Clarence might shout again, but he did not. He was well on his way towards home with Tommy and Ruby when Laura shut the shanty door behind her and Almanzo tucked her again into the cutter.

7

A Knife in the Dark

The third week went by, and the fourth. Now there were only four weeks more. Though every morning Laura was anxious about the school day ahead, still it was not as bad as the Brewsters' house, and every afternoon at four o'clock she drew a breath of relief; one more day had gone well.

There were no blizzards yet, but February was very cold. The wind was like knives. Every Friday and Sunday, Almanzo Wilder had made the long, cold drive, to take her home. Laura did not know how she could get through the week, without looking forward to Saturday at home. But she felt sorry for Almanzo, who was making those cold drives for nothing.

Much as she wanted to go home every week, she did not want to be under such an obligation to anyone. She was going with him only to get home, but he did not know that. Perhaps he was expecting her to go driving with him after she went home to stay. She did not want to feel obliged to go with him, neither could she be unfair, or deceitful. She felt that she must explain this to him, but she did not know how.

At home, Ma worried because she was thinner. 'Are you sure you get enough to eat at Brewster's?' Ma asked, and Laura answered, 'Oh, yes, a great plenty! But it doesn't taste like home cooking.'

Pa said, 'You know, Laura, you don't *have* to finish the term. If anything worries you too much, you can always come home.'

'Why, Pa!' Laura said, 'I couldn't *quit*. I wouldn't get another certificate. Besides, it's only three weeks more.'

'I'm afraid you're studying too hard,' Ma said. 'You don't look like you get enough sleep.'

'I go to bed every night at eight o'clock,' Laura assured her.

'Well, as you say, it's only three weeks more,' said Ma.

No one knew how she dreaded to go back to Mrs Brewster's. It would do no good to tell them. Being at home every Saturday raised her spirits and gave her courage for another week. Still, it was not fair to take so much from Almanzo Wilder.

He was driving her out to the Brewsters' that Sunday afternoon. They hardly ever spoke during those long drives; it was too cold to talk. The jingling sleigh bells sounded frosty in the sparkling cold, and the light cutter sped so fast that the north wind following it was not very sharp on their backs. But he must face that wind all the way back to town.

The Brewsters' shanty was not far ahead when Laura said to herself: 'Stop shilly-shallying!' Then she spoke out. She said, 'I am going with you only because I want to get home. When I am home to stay, I will not go with you any more. So now you know, and if you want to save yourself these long, cold drives, you can.'

The words sounded horrid to her as she said them. They were abrupt and rude and hateful. At the same time, a dreadful realization swept over her, of what it would mean if Almanzo did not come for her again. She would have to spend Saturdays and Sundays with Mrs Brewster.

After a startled moment, Almanzo said slowly, 'I see.'

There was no time to say more. They were at Mrs Brewster's door, and the horses must not stand and get chilled. Quickly Laura got out, saying, 'Thank you.' He touched his hand to his fur cap and the cutter went swiftly away.

'It is only three weeks more,' Laura said to herself, but she could not keep her spirits from sinking.

All that week the weather grew colder. On Thursday morning Laura found that the quilt had frozen stiff around her nose while she slept. Her fingers were so numb that she could hardly dress. In the other room the stove lids were red hot, but the heat seemed unable to penetrate the cold around it.

Laura was holding her numbed hands above the stove when Mr Brewster burst in, tore off his boots, and began violently rubbing his feet. Mrs Brewster went quickly to him.

'Oh, Lewis, what's the matter?' she asked so anxiously that Laura was surprised.

'My feet,' Mr Brewster said. 'I ran all the way from the schoolhouse but there's no feeling in them.'

'Let me help,' his wife said. She took his feet into her lap and helped him rub them. She was so concerned and so kind that she seemed like another woman. 'Oh, Lewis, this dreadful country!' she said. 'Oh, am I hurting you?'

'Go on,' Mr Brewster grunted. 'It shows the blood's coming back into them.'

When they had saved his half-frozen feet, Mr Brewster told Laura not to go to school that day. 'You would freeze,' he said.

She protested, 'But the children will come, and I must be there.'

'I don't think they'll come,' he said. 'I built a fire, and if they do come, they can get warm and go home again. There will be no school today,' he said flatly.

That settled it, for a teacher must obey the head of the school board.

It was a long, wretched day. Mrs Brewster sat huddled in a quilt, close to the stove, and sullenly brooding. Mr Brewster's feet were painful, and Johnny fretted with a feverish cold. Laura did the dishes, made her bed in the freezing cold, and studied her schoolbooks. When she tried to talk, there was something menacing in Mrs Brewster's silence.

At last it was bedtime. Laura hoped desperately that tomorrow she could go to school; meantime, she could escape by going to sleep. The cold in the bedroom took her breath away and stiffened her hands so she could hardly undress. For a long time she lay too cold to sleep, but slowly she began to be warmer.

A scream woke her. Mrs Brewster screamed, 'You kicked me!'

'I did not,' Mr Brewster said. 'But I will, if you don't put away that butcher knife.'

Laura sat straight up. Moonlight was streaming over her bed from the window. Mrs Brewster screamed again, a wild sound without words that made Laura's scalp crinkle.

'Take that knife back to the kitchen,' Mr Brewster said.

Laura peeped through the crack between the curtains. The moonlight shone through the calico, and thinned the darkness so that Laura saw Mrs Brewster standing there. Her long white flannel nightgown trailed on the floor and her black hair fell loose over her shoulders. In her upraised hand she held the butcher knife. Laura had never been so terribly frightened.

'If I can't go home one way, I can another,' said Mrs Brewster.

'Go put that knife back,' said Mr Brewster. He lay still, but tensed to spring.

'Will you or won't you?' she demanded.

'You'll catch your death of cold,' he said. 'I won't go over that again, this time of night. I've got you and Johnny to support, and nothing in the world but this claim. Put away that knife and come to bed before you freeze.'

The knife stopped shaking, as Mrs Brewster's fist clenched on the handle.

'Go put it back in the kitchen,' Mr Brewster ordered.

After a moment, Mrs Brewster turned and went to the kitchen. Not until she came back and got into bed did Laura let the curtains fall together again. Softly she drew the bedcovers over her and lay staring at the curtain. She was terribly frightened. She dared not sleep. Suppose she woke to see Mrs Brewster standing over her with that knife? Mrs Brewster did not like her.

What could she do? The nearest house was a mile away; she would freeze if she tried to reach it in this cold. Wide awake, she stared at the curtains and listened. There was no sound but the wind. The moon went down, and she stared at the dark until the grey winter daylight came. When she heard Mr Brewster build the fire and Mrs Brewster beginning to cook breakfast, she got up and dressed.

Nothing was different; breakfast was the usual silent meal. Laura went to school as soon as she could get away. She felt safe there, for the day. It was Friday.

The wind was blowing fiercely. Fortunately it was not a blizzard wind, but it scoured hard particles of snow from the frozen drifts and drove them through every crack in the shanty's north and west walls. From all sides the cold came in. The big coal heater seemed to make no impression on that cold.

Laura called the school to order. Though she was near the stove, her feet were numb and her fingers could not grip a pencil. She knew that it was colder in the seats.

'Better put your coats on again,' she said, 'and all of

you come to the fire. You may take turns sitting in the front seat or standing by the stove to get warm. Study as best you can.'

All day the snow was blown low across the prairie, and through the schoolroom's walls. Ice froze thick on the water pail, and at noon they set their dinner pails on the stove to thaw the frozen food before they ate it. The wind was steadily growing colder.

It cheered Laura to see how well every pupil behaved. Not one took advantage of the disorder to be idle or unruly. No one whispered. They all stood by the stove, studying, and quietly turning about to warm their backs, and all their answers were good. Charles and Clarence took turns, going out into the wind to get coal from the bin and keep up the fire.

Laura dreaded the day's end. She was afraid to go back to the house. She was sleepy; she knew that she must sleep, and she feared to sleep in Mrs Brewster's house. All day tomorrow and Sunday she must be in that house with Mrs Brewster, and much of the time Mr Brewster would be at the stable.

She knew that she must not be afraid. Pa had always said that she must never be afraid. Very likely, nothing would happen. She was not exactly afraid of Mrs Brewster, for she knew that she was quick, and strong as a little French horse. That is, when she was awake. But she had never wanted so much to go home.

It had been right to tell Almanzo Wilder the truth, but she wished that she had not done it so soon. Still, he would not have come so far in such bitter cold, anyway. Every moment the wind blew stronger, and colder.

At half past three they were all so cold that she thought of dismissing school early. The mile that Martha and Charles must walk worried her. On the other hand, she could not cut short the pupils' opportunity for learning, and this was not a blizzard.

Suddenly she heard sleigh bells. They were coming! In a moment they were at the door. Prince and Lady passed the window, and Clarence exclaimed, 'That Wilder's a bigger fool than I thought he was to come out in this weather!'

'You may all put away your books,' Laura said. It was much too cold for the horses to stand outdoors. 'It is growing colder, and the sooner everyone reaches home, the better,' she said. 'School is dismissed.'

8

A Cold Ride

'Careful of the lantern,' was all that Almanzo said as he helped her into the cutter. Several horse blankets were spread over the seat, and on their ends, under the fur buffalo robes, a lantern stood burning to warm the nest for Laura's feet.

When she ran into the house, Mr Brewster said, 'You aren't thinking of such a thing as driving in this cold?'

'Yes,' she answered. She lost no time. In the bedroom, she buttoned on her other flannel petticoat, and pulled over her shoes her other pair of woollen stockings. She doubled her thick black woollen veil and wrapped it twice around her face and hood, and wound its long ends around her throat. Over that she put her muffler, crossed its ends on her chest, and buttoned her coat over all. She ran out to the cutter.

Mr Brewster was there, protesting. 'You folks are fools to try it,' he said. 'It is not safe. I want him to put up here for the night,' he said to Laura.

'Think you'd better not risk it?' Almanzo asked her.

'Are you going back?' she asked him.

'Yes, I've got stock to take care of,' he said.

'Then I'm going,' she said.

Prince and Lady started swiftly into the wind. It struck through all the woollen folds and took Laura's breath away. She bent her head into it, but she felt it flowing like icy water on her cheeks and chest. Her teeth clenched to keep from chattering.

The horses were eager to go. Their trotting feet drummed on the hard snow and every sleigh bell cheerily rang. Laura was thankful for the speed that would soon let them reach shelter from the cold. She was sorry when

they trotted more slowly. They dropped into a walk, and she supposed that Almanzo was slowing them for a rest. Probably horses must not be driven too hard against such a bitter wind.

She was surprised when he stopped them, and got out of the cutter. Dimly through the black veil she saw him going to their drooping heads, and she heard him say, 'Just a minute, Lady,' as he laid his mittened hands on Prince's nose. After a moment he took his hands away with a scraping motion, and Prince tossed his head high and shook music from his bells. Quickly Almanzo did the same thing to Lady's nose, and she, too, tossed up her head. Almanzo tucked himself into the cutter and they sped on.

Laura's veil was a slab of frost against her mouth that made speaking uncomfortable, so she said nothing, but she wondered. Almanzo's fur cap came down to his eyebrows, and his muffler covered his face to his eyes. His breath froze white on the fur and along the muffler's edge. He drove with one hand, keeping the other under the robes, and often changing so that neither hand would freeze.

The horses trotted more slowly again, and again he got out and went to hold his hands on their noses. When he came back Laura asked him, 'What's the matter?'

He answered, 'Their breath freezes over their noses till they can't breath. Have to thaw it off.'

They said no more. Laura remembered the cattle drifting in the October blizzard that began the Hard

Winter; their breath had smothered them, till they would have died if Pa had not broken the ice from their noses.

The cold was piercing through the buffalo robes. It crept through Laura's wool coat and woollen dress, through all her flannel petticoats and the two pairs of woollen stockings drawn over the folded legs of her warm flannel union suit. In spite of the heat from the lantern, her feet and her legs grew cold. Her clenched jaws ached, and two sharp little aches began at her temples.

Almanzo reached across and pulled the robes higher, tucking them behind her elbows.

'Cold?' he asked.

'No,' Laura answered clearly. It was all she could say without letting her teeth chatter. It was not true, but he knew that she meant she was not so cold that she could not bear it. There was nothing to do but go on, and she knew that he was cold, too.

Again he stopped the horses and got out into the wind, to thaw the ice from their noses. Again the bells rang out merrily. The sound seemed as cruel, now, as the merciless wind. Though her veil made a darkness, she could see that the sun was shining bright on the white prairie.

Almanzo came back into the cutter.

'All right?' he asked.

'Yes,' she said.

'I've got to stop every couple of miles. They can't make more,' he explained.

Laura's heart sank. Then they had come only six miles. There were still six miles to go. They went on swiftly against the cutting wind. In spite of all she could do, Laura shook all over. Pressing her knees tight together did not stop their shaking. The lantern beside her feet under the fur robes seemed to give no warmth. The pains bored into her temples, and a knot of pain tightened in her middle.

It seemed a long time before the horses slowed again, and again Almanzo stopped them. The bells rang out, first Prince's, then Lady's. Almanzo was clumsy, getting into the cutter again.

'You all right?' he asked.

'Yes,' she said.

She was growing more used to the cold. It did not hurt so much. Only the pain in her middle kept tightening, but it was duller. The sound of the wind and the bells and the cutter's runners on the snow all blended into one monotonous sound, rather pleasant. She knew when Almanzo left the cutter to thaw the ice from the horses' noses again, but everything seemed like a dream.

'All right?' he asked. She nodded. It was too much trouble to speak.

'Laura!' he said, taking hold of her shoulder and shaking her a little. The shaking hurt; it made her feel the cold again. 'You sleepy?'

'A little,' she answered.

'Don't go to sleep. You hear me?'

'I won't,' she said. She knew what he meant. If you go to sleep in such cold, you freeze to death.

The horses stopped again. Almanzo asked, 'Making it all right?'

'Yes,' she said. He went to take the ice from the horses' noses. When he came back he said, 'It's not far now.'

She knew he wanted her to answer. She said, 'That's good.'

Sleepiness kept coming over her in long, warm waves, though she was holding her eyes wide open. She shook her head and took burning gulps of air, and struggled awake, but another wave of sleepiness came, and another. Often when she was too tired to struggle any longer, Almanzo's voice helped her. She heard him ask, 'All right?'

'Yes,' she said, and for a moment she would be awake; she heard the sleigh bells clearly and felt the wind blowing. Then another wave came.

'Here we are!' she heard him say.

'Yes,' she answered. Then suddenly she knew that they were at the back door of home. The wind was not so strong here; its force was broken by the building on the other side of Second Street. Almanzo lifted the robes and she tried to get out of the cutter, but she was too stiff; she could not stand up.

The door flashed open, and Ma took hold of her, exclaiming, 'My goodness! are you frozen?'

'I'm afraid she's pretty cold,' Almanzo said.

'Get those horses into shelter before they freeze,' Pa said. 'We'll take care of her.'

The sleigh bells dashed away while, with Pa and Ma holding her arms, Laura stumbled into the kitchen.

'Take off her shoes, Carrie,' Ma said as she peeled off Laura's veil and knitted woollen hood. The frost of her breath had frozen the veil to the hood and they came away together. 'Your face is red,' Ma said in relief. 'I'm thankful it isn't white and frozen.'

'I'm only numb,' Laura said. Her feet were not frozen, either, though she could hardly feel Pa's hands rubbing them. Now in the warm room she began to shake from head to foot and her teeth chattered. She sat close by the stove while she drank the hot ginger tea that Ma made for her. But she could not get warm.

She had been cold so long, ever since she got out of bed that morning. In the Brewsters' cold kitchen her place at the table was farthest from the stove and near the window. Then came the long walk through the snow to school, with the wind blowing against her and whirling up under her skirts; the long, cold day in the schoolhouse, and then the long ride home. But there was nothing to complain of, for now she was at home.

'You took a long chance, Laura,' Pa said soberly. 'I did not know that Wilder was starting until he had gone, and then I was sure he'd stay at Brewster's. It was forty below zero when that crazy fellow started, and the thermometer froze soon afterwards. It has been steadily growing colder ever since; there's no telling how cold it is now.'

'All's well that ends well, Pa,' Laura answered him with a shaky laugh.

It seemed to her that she never would get warm. But it was wonderful to eat supper in the happy kitchen, and then to sleep safely in her own bed. She woke to find the weather moderating; at breakfast Pa said that the temperature was near twenty below zero. The cold snap was over.

In church that Sunday morning Laura thought how foolish she had been to let herself be so miserable and frightened. There were only two weeks more, and then she could come home to stay.

While Almanzo was driving her out to the Brewsters' that afternoon she thanked him for taking her home that week.

'No need for thanks,' he said. 'You knew I would.'

'Why, no, I didn't,' she answered honestly.

'What do you take me for?' he asked. 'Do you think I'm the kind of a fellow that'd leave you out there at Brewster's when you're so homesick, just because there's nothing in it for me?'

'Why, I . . .' Laura stopped. The truth was that she had never thought much about what kind of a person he was. He was so much older; he was a homesteader.

'To tell you the whole truth,' he said, 'I was in two

minds about risking that trip. I figured all week I'd drive out for you, but when I looked at the thermometer I came pretty near deciding against it.'

'Why didn't you?' Laura asked.

'Well, I was starting out in the cutter, and I pulled up in front of Fuller's to look at the thermometer. The mercury was all down in the bulb, below forty, and the wind blowing colder every minute. Just then Cap Garland came by. He saw me there, ready to go out to Brewster's for you, and looking at the thermometer. So he looked at it and you know how he grins? Well, as he was going on into Fuller's, he just said to me over his shoulder, "God hates a coward."'

'So you came because you wouldn't take a dare?' Laura asked.

'No, it wasn't a dare,' Almanzo said. 'I just figured he was right.'

9

The Superintendent's Visit

'I have only to get through one day at a time,' Laura thought, when she went into the house. Everything was still all wrong there. Mrs Brewster did not speak; Johnny was always miserable, and Mr Brewster stayed at the stable as much as he could. That evening while she studied, Laura made four marks on her notebook, for Monday, Tuesday, Wednesday, Thursday. She would mark off one of them every night; when they were gone, there would be only one week more.

Day after day the weather grew colder again, but still there was no blizzard. The nights passed quietly, though Laura lay half-asleep and woke often. Each evening she crossed out a mark. It seemed to make time pass more quickly, to look forward to crossing out one more day.

All Wednesday night she heard the wind howling and snow beating on the window. She dreaded that there might be no school next day. But in the morning the sun was shining, though there was no warmth in it. A bitter wind rolled the snow low across the prairie. Laura gladly faced it as she fought her way to the school shanty, breaking her path again.

Snow was blowing through the cracks, and once more she let her pupils stand by the stove to study. But slowly the red-hot stove warmed the room, until at recess Laura could hardly see her breath when she blew it above Clarence's back seat. So when she called the school to order she said, 'The room is warmer now. You may take your seats.'

They were hardly in their places, when a sudden knock sounded on the door. Who could it be? she wondered. As she hurried to the door, she glanced through the window, but nothing was to be seen. At the door stood Mr Williams, the county superintendent of schools.

His blanketed team stood tied to a corner of the school shanty. The soft snow had muffled the sounds of their coming, and they had no bells.

This was the test of Laura's teaching, and how thankful she was that the pupils were in their seats. Mr Williams smiled pleasantly as she gave him her chair by the red-hot stove. Every pupil bent studiously to work, but Laura could feel how alert and tense they were. She was so nervous that it was hard to keep her voice low and steady.

It heartened her, that each one tried hard to do his best for her. Even Charles made an effort, and surpassed himself. Mr Williams sat listening to answer after answer, while the wind blew low and loud and the snow drifted through the cracks in the walls.

Charles raised his hand and asked, 'Please may I come to the stove to warm?' Laura said that he might, and without thinking to ask permission, Martha came too. They were studying from the same book. When their hands were warm, they went back to their seat, quietly, but without asking permission. It did not speak well for Laura's discipline.

Just before noon, Mr Williams said that he must go. Then Laura must ask him if he wished to speak to the school.

'Yes, I do,' he answered grimly, and as he rose to his full height of six feet, Laura's heart stood still. Desperately she wondered what she had done that was wrong.

With his head nearly touching the ceiling he stood silent a moment, to emphasize what he intended to say. Then he spoke.

'Whatever else you do, *keep your feet warm.*'

He smiled at them all, and again at Laura, and after shaking her hand warmly, he was gone.

At noon Clarence emptied the coal hod into the stove, and went out into the cold to fill it again at the bin. As he came back he said, 'We'll need more coal on the fire before night. It's getting colder, fast.'

They all gathered close to the stove to eat their cold lunches. When Laura called the school to order she told them to bring their books to the fire. 'You may stand by the stove or move about as you please. So long as you are quiet and learn your lessons, we will let that be the rule as long as this cold weather lasts.'

The plan worked well. Lessons went better than ever before, and the room was quiet while they all studied and kept their feet warm.

10

Almanzo says Good-bye

That Saturday at home, Ma was worried about Laura. 'Are you coming down with something?' she asked. 'It isn't like you to sit half-asleep.'

'I feel a little tired. It isn't anything, Ma,' Laura said.

Pa looked up from his paper. 'That Clarence making trouble again?'

'Oh, no, Pa! He's doing splendidly, and they are all as good as can be.' She was not exactly lying, but she could not tell them about Mrs Brewster and the knife. If they knew, they would not let her go back, and she must finish her school. A teacher could not walk away and leave a term of school unfinished. If she did, she would not deserve another certificate, and no school board would hire her.

So she made a greater effort to hide from them her sleepiness and her dread of going back to Mrs Brewster's house. There was only one more week.

By Sunday afternoon the weather had moderated. The temperature was only fifteen degrees below zero when Laura and Almanzo set out. There was hardly any wind and the sun shone brightly.

Out of a silence Laura said, 'Only one more week, and I'll be so glad when it's over.'

'Maybe you will miss the sleigh rides?' Almanzo suggested.

'This one is nice,' Laura said. 'But mostly it is so cold. I should think you'd be glad not to drive so far any more. I don't know why you ever started making these long drives; you didn't need to take them to get home, the way I do.'

'Oh, sometimes a fellow gets tired of sitting around,' Almanzo replied. 'Two old bachelors get pretty dull by themselves.'

'Why, there are lots of people in town! You and your brother needn't stay by yourselves,' Laura said.

'There hasn't been anything going on in town since the school exhibition,' Almanzo objected. 'All a fellow can do is hang around the saloon playing pool, or in one of the stores watching the draughts players. Sometimes he'd rather be out with better company, even if it does get cold, driving.'

Laura had not thought of herself as good company. If that was what he wanted, she thought, she should make an effort to be more entertaining. But she could not think of anything entertaining to say. She tried to think of something, while she watched the sleek brown horses, trotting so swiftly.

Their dainty feet spurned the snow in perfect rhythm, and their blue shadows flew along the snow beside them.

They were so gay, tossing their heads to make a chiming of the bells, pricking their ears forward and back, lifting their noses to the breeze of their speed that rippled their black manes. Laura drew a deep breath and exclaimed, 'How beautiful!'

'What is beautiful?' Almanzo asked.

'The horses. Look at them!' Laura answered. At that moment, Prince and Lady touched noses as though they whispered to each other, then together they tried to break into a run.

When Almanzo had gently but firmly pulled them into a trot again, he asked, 'How would you like to drive them?'

'Oh!' Laura cried. But she had to add, honestly, 'Pa won't let me drive his horses. He says I am too little and would get hurt.'

'Prince and Lady wouldn't hurt anybody,' Almanzo said. 'I raised them myself. But if you think they're beautiful, I wish you could've seen the first horse I ever raised, Starlight. I named him for the white star on his forehead.'

His father had given him Starlight as a colt, back in York State when he was nine years old. He told Laura all about gentling Starlight, and breaking him, and what a beautiful horse he was. Starlight had come west to Minnesota, and when first Almanzo came out to the western prairies, he had come riding Starlight. Starlight was nine years old then, when Almanzo rode him back to

85

Marshall, Minnesota, one hundred and five miles in one day, and Starlight came in so fresh that he tried to race another horse at the journey's end.

'Where is he now?' Laura asked.

'At pasture on Father's farm back in Minnesota,' Almanzo told her. 'He is not as young as he used to be, and I need a double team for driving out here, so I gave him back to Father.'

The time had passed so quickly that Laura was surprised to see the Brewsters' ahead. She tried to keep up her courage, but her heart sank.

'What makes you so quiet, so sudden?' Almanzo asked.

'I was wishing we were going in the opposite direction,' Laura said.

'We'll be doing that next Friday.' He slowed the horses. 'We can delay it a little,' he said, and she knew that somehow he understood how she dreaded going into that house.

'Till next Friday, then,' he smiled encouragingly, as he drove away.

Day by day and night by night that week went by, until there was only one more night to get through. Tomorrow was Friday, the last day of school. When that one night and day were over, she would go home to stay.

She so dreaded that something might happen, this last night. Often she woke with a start, but all was quiet and her heart slowly ceased thumping.

Friday's lessons were unusually well-learned, and every pupil was carefully well-behaved.

When afternoon recess was over, Laura called the school to order, and said there would be no more lessons. School would be dismissed early, because this was the last day.

She knew that she must make some closing speech to the school, so she praised them all for the work they had done. 'You have made good use of the opportunity you had to come to school,' she told them.

'I hope that each of you can get more schooling, but if you cannot, you can study at home as Lincoln did. An education is worth striving for, and if you can not have much help in getting one, you can each help yourself to an education if you try.'

Then she gave Ruby one of her name-cards, of thin, pale pink cardboard with a spray of roses and cornflowers curving above her printed name. On the back she had written, 'Presented to Ruby Brewster, by her teacher, with kind regards. Brewster School, February 1883.'

Tommy was next, then Martha and Charles, and Clarence. They were all so pleased. Laura let them have a moment to enjoy looking at the pretty cards, and carefully place them in their books. Then she told them to make ready their books, slates, and pencils, to carry home. For the last time she said, 'School is dismissed.'

She had never been more surprised than she was then.

For instead of putting on their wraps as she expected, they all came up to her desk. Martha gave her a beautiful, red apple. Ruby shyly gave her a little cake that her mother had baked for her gift. And Tommy and Charles and Clarence each gave her a new pencil that he had carefully sharpened for her.

She hardly knew how to thank them, but Martha said, 'It's us, I mean we, that thank you, Miss Ingalls. Thank you for helping me with grammar.' 'Thank you, Miss Ingalls,' Ruby said. 'I wish it had frosting on it.' The boys did not say anything, but after they had all said good-bye and gone, Clarence came back.

Standing by Laura's table and leaning against it he looked down at his cap in his hands and muttered, 'I'm sorry I was so mean.'

'Why, Clarence! That's all right!' Laura exclaimed. 'And you have done wonderfully well in your studies. I am proud of you.'

He looked at her with his old saucy grin, and shot out of the room, slamming the door so that the shanty shook.

Laura cleaned the blackboard and swept the floor. She stacked her books and papers and shut the draughts of the stove. Then she put on her hood and coat and stood at the window waiting until the sleigh bells came jingling and Prince and Lady stopped at the door.

School was out. She was going home to stay! Her heart was so light that she felt like singing with the sleigh bells, and fast as the horses trotted, they seemed slow.

'You won't get there any faster, pushing,' Almanzo said once, and she laughed aloud to find that she was pushing her feet hard against the cutter's dashboard. But he did not talk much, and neither did she. It was enough to be going home.

Not until she had thanked him nicely and said good night and was in the sitting room taking off her wraps, did she remember that he had not said, 'Good night.' He had not said, 'I'll see you Sunday afternoon,' as he had always said before. He had said, 'Good-bye.'

Of course, she thought. It was good-bye. This had been the last sleigh ride.

11

Jingle Bells

Waking next morning was happier than Christmas. 'Oh, I'm at home!' Laura thought. She called, 'Carrie! Good morning! Wake up, sleepyhead!' She almost laughed with joy as she shivered into her dress and skipped downstairs to button her shoes and comb her hair in the warming kitchen where Ma was getting breakfast.

'Good morning, Ma!' she sang.

'Good morning,' Ma smiled. 'I declare you look better already.'

'It's nice to be home,' Laura said. 'Now what shall I do first?'

She was busy all that morning, helping with Saturday's work. Though usually she disliked the dryness of flour on her hands, today she enjoyed kneading the bread, thinking happily that she would be at home to eat the fresh, brown-crusted loaves. Her heart sang with the song on her lips; she was not going back to the Brewsters' ever again.

It was a beautifully sunny day, and that afternoon when the work was all done, Laura hoped that Mary Power would come to talk to her while they crocheted. Ma was gently rocking while she knitted by the sunny window, Carrie was piecing her patchwork, but somehow Laura could not settle down. Mary did not come, and Laura had just decided that she would put on her wraps and go to see Mary, when she heard sleigh bells.

For some reason, her heart jumped. But the bells rang thinly as they sped by. There were only a few bells; they were not the rich strings of bells that Prince and Lady wore. Their music had not died away, when again sleigh bells went tinkling past. Then all up and down the street, the stillness sparkled with the ringing of the little bells.

Laura went to the window. She saw Minnie Johnson and Fred Gilbert flash by, then Arthur Johnson with a girl that Laura did not know. The full music of double strings of bells came swiftly, and Mary Power and Cap Garland dashed by in a cutter. So that was what Mary was doing. Cap Garland had a cutter and full strings of sleigh bells, too. More and more laughing couples drove up and down the street, in sleighs and cutters, passing and repassing the window where Laura stood.

At last she sat soberly down to her crocheting. The sitting room was neat and quiet. Nobody came to see Laura. She had been gone so long that probably no one thought of her. All that afternoon the sleigh bells were going by. Up and down the street her schoolmates went laughing in the sunny cold, having such a good time.

Again and again Mary and Cap sped past, in a cutter made for two.

Well, Laura thought, tomorrow she would see Ida at Sunday School. But Ida did not come to church that Sunday; Mrs Brown said that she had a bad cold.

That Sunday afternoon the weather was even more beautiful. Again the sleigh bells were ringing, and laughter floating on the wind. Again Mary Power and Cap went by, and Minnie and Fred, and Frank Harthorn and May Bird, and all the newcomers whom Laura barely knew. Two by two they went gaily by, laughing and singing with the chiming bells. No one remembered Laura. She had been away so long that everyone had forgotten her.

Soberly she tried to read Tennyson's poems. She tried not to mind being forgotten and left out. She tried not to hear the sleigh bells and the laughter, but more and more she felt that she could not bear it.

Suddenly, a ringing of bells stopped at the door! Before Pa could look up from his paper, Laura had the door open, and there stood Prince and Lady with the little cutter, and Almanzo stood beside it smiling.

'Would you like to go sleigh riding?' he asked.

'Oh, yes!' Laura answered. 'Just a minute, I'll put on my wraps.'

Quickly she got into her coat and put on her white hood and mittens. Almanzo tucked her into the cutter and they sped away.

'I didn't know your eyes were so blue,' Almanzo said.

'It's my white hood,' Laura told him. 'I always wore my dark one to Brewster's.' She gave a gasp, and laughed aloud.

'What's so funny?' Almanzo asked, smiling.

'It's a joke on me,' Laura said. 'I didn't intend to go with you any more but I forgot. Why did you come?'

'I thought maybe you'd change your mind after you watched the crowd go by,' Almanzo answered. Then they laughed together.

Theirs was one of the line of sleighs and cutters, swiftly going the length of Main Street, swinging in a circle on the prairie to the south, then speeding up Main Street and around in a circle to the north, and back again, and again. Far and wide the sunshine sparkled on the snowy land; the wind blew cold against their faces. The sleigh bells were ringing, the sleigh runners squeaking on the hard-packed snow, and Laura was so happy that she had to sing:

> 'Jingle bells, jingle bells,
> Jingle all the way!
> Oh what fun it is to ride
> In a one-horse open sleigh.'

All along the speeding line, other voices took up the tune. Swinging out on the open prairie and back, fast up

the street and out on the prairie and back again, the bells went ringing and the voices singing in the frosty air.

> 'Jingle bells, jingle bells,
> Jingle all the way!'

They were quite safe from blizzards because they did not go far from town. The wind was blowing, but not too hard, and everyone was so happy and gay for it was only twenty degrees below zero and the sun shone.

12

East or West, Home is Best

Gladly Laura set out to school with Carrie Monday morning. As they picked their way across the icy ruts of the street, Carrie said with a happy sigh, 'It's good to be walking to school together again. It never seemed right without you.'

'I feel the same way,' Laura answered.

When they went into the schoolhouse, Ida exclaimed joyfully, 'Hello, Teacher!' and everyone turned from the stove to gather around Laura. 'How does it seem to be coming to school yourself?' Ida asked; her nose was swollen and red from the cold, but her brown eyes were gay as ever.

'It seems *good*,' Laura answered, squeezing Ida's hand while all the others welcomed her back. Even Nellie Oleson seemed friendly.

'Quite a few sleigh rides you've been having,' Nellie said. 'Now you're home again, maybe you'll take some of us with you.'

Laura only answered, 'Maybe.' She wondered what Nellie was scheming now. Then Mr Owen left his desk and came to greet Laura.

'We are glad to have you with us again,' he said. 'I hear you did well with your school.'

'Thank you, sir,' she answered. 'I am glad to be back.' She wanted to ask who had spoken to him about her teaching, but of course she did not.

The morning began a little anxiously, for she feared that she might be behind her class, but she found that she had more than kept up with it. The lessons were all reviews of those that she had learned during the wretched evenings at the Brewsters'. She knew them perfectly; she was still sailing at the head of the class with flying colours, and she was feeling happily confident until the morning recess.

Then the girls began to talk about their compositions, and Laura discovered that Mr Owen had told the grammar class to write, for that day's lesson, a composition on 'Ambition'.

The grammar class would be called upon immediately after recess. Laura was in a panic. She had never written a composition, and now she must do in a few minutes what the others had been working at since yesterday. They had all written their compositions at home, and Mrs Brown had helped Ida write hers. Mrs Brown wrote for the church papers, so Ida's composition would be good.

Laura had no idea how to begin. She knew nothing about ambition. The only thought in her head was that she was going to fail in a class that she had always led. She must not fail, she couldn't. She would not. But how did one write a composition? Only five minutes were left.

She found herself staring at the yellow leather cover of the dictionary on its stand by Mr Owen's desk. Perhaps, she thought, she might get an idea from reading the definition of ambition. Her fingers were chilly as she hurriedly turned the 'A' pages, but the definition was interesting. Back at her desk, she wrote as fast as she could, and kept on writing desperately while the school was called to order. Miserably she felt that her composition was not good, but there was no time to write it again nor to add anything more. Mr Owen was calling the grammar class.

One by one, as he called upon them, the others read their compositions, while Laura's heart sank. Each one seemed better than her own. At last Mr Owen said, 'Laura Ingalls,' and all the class rustled as everyone looked at her expectantly.

Laura stood up, and made herself read aloud what she had written. It was the best that she had been able to do.

AMBITION

Ambition is necessary to accomplishment. Without an ambition to gain an end, nothing would be done. Without

98

an ambition to excel others and to surpass one's self there would be no superior merit. To win anything, we must have the ambition to do so.

Ambition is a good servant but a bad master. So long as we control our ambition, it is good, but if there is danger of our being ruled by it, then I would say in the words of Shakespeare, 'Cromwell, I charge thee, fling away ambition. By that sin fell the angels.'

That was all. Laura stood miserably waiting for Mr Owen's comment. He looked at her sharply and said, 'You have written compositions before?'

'No, sir,' Laura said. 'This is my first.'

'Well, you should write more of them, I would not have believed that anyone could do so well the first time,' Mr Owen told her.

Laura stammered in astonishment. 'It is s . . . so short . . . It is mostly from the dictionary . . .'

'It is not much like the dictionary,' Mr Owen said. 'There are no corrections. It grades one hundred. Class is dismissed.'

It couldn't be marked higher. Laura still was at the head of her class. She felt confident now that with steady work she would keep her place at the head of her classes, and she looked forward happily to writing more compositions.

Time no longer dragged. That week went by in a flash, and on Friday when Laura and Carrie went home to dinner

Pa said, 'I have something for you, Laura.'

His eyes were twinkling as he drew his pocketbook from his pocket. Then one by one he laid in her hand four ten-dollar bills.

'I saw Brewster this morning,' Pa explained. 'He gave me this for you, and said you taught a good school. They would like to have you back next winter. But I told him you wouldn't go so far from home again in the wintertime. I know it wasn't pleasant at Brewster's even if you didn't complain, and I'm proud that you stuck it out, Laura.'

'Oh, Pa! It was worth it,' Laura said breathlessly. 'Forty dollars!'

She had known that she was earning forty dollars, but the bills in her hand made the fact seem real for the first time. She looked at them, hardly able to believe it even now. Four ten-dollar bills; forty dollars.

Then she held it out to Pa. 'Here, Pa. Take it and keep it for Mary. It's enough so that she can come home on her vacation this summer, isn't it?'

'Plenty for that, and then some,' said Pa, as he folded the bills again into his pocketbook.

'Oh, Laura, aren't you going to have anything at all for teaching your school?' Carrie exclaimed.

'We'll all see Mary this summer,' Laura answered happily. 'I was only teaching school for Mary.' It was a wonderful feeling, to know that she had helped so much. Forty dollars. As she sat down to the good dinner in the pleasant kitchen of home, she said, 'I wish I could earn some more.'

'You can if you want to,' Ma said unexpectedly. 'Mrs McKee said this morning she would like to have you help her on Saturdays. She has more dressmaking than she can do alone, and she will pay you fifty cents and dinner.'

'Oh!' Laura cried out. 'Did you tell her I will, Ma?'

'I said you might if you'd like to,' Ma smiled.

'When? Tomorrow?' Laura eagerly asked.

'Tomorrow morning at eight o'clock,' said Ma. 'Mrs McKee said she wouldn't be ready for you till that late. Only from eight to six, she said, unless there's a rush, and she'll give you your supper if you stay to finish up something in the evening.'

Mrs McKee was the town's dressmaker. The McKees were newcomers who lived in a new house, between Clancy's dry-goods store and the new office building at the corner of Main and Second Street. Laura had met Mrs McKee at church, and liked her. She was tall and slender with kind blue eyes and a pleasant smile. Her light brown hair was worn in a knot at the back of her head.

So now Laura's time was full, and all of it was pleasant. The crowded days at school went swiftly by, and all the week Laura looked forward to the day of sewing busily in Mrs McKee's living room – that was always in such spotless order that Laura hardly noticed the cook-stove at one end.

On Sunday morning there was Sunday School and church, and every pleasant Sunday afternoon there was the sleigh-ride party. Prince and Lady came down the street with their full strings of sweet-toned bells gaily ringing, and stopped at the door for Laura, and she went with Almanzo in the little cutter behind the prettiest and fastest-stepping horses in the Sunday parade.

But best of all were the mornings and the evenings at home. Laura realized that she had never appreciated them until now. There were no sullen silences, no smouldering quarrels, no ugly outbreaks of anger.

Instead there was work with pleasant talk, there were happy little jokes and evenings of cosy studying and reading, and the music of Pa's fiddle. How good it was to hear the old familiar tunes as the fiddle sang them in the warm, lamplighted room of home. Often Laura thought how happy and how fortunate she was. Nothing anywhere could be better than being at home with the home folks, she was sure.

13
Springtime

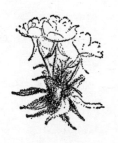

On a Friday afternoon in April Laura and Ida and Mary Power walked slowly home from school. The air was soft and moist, the eaves were dripping, and the snow was slushy underfoot.

'Spring is almost here again,' Ida said. 'Only three more weeks of school.'

'Yes, and then we'll be moving out to the claim again,' said Mary. 'You will, too, Laura, won't you?'

'I suppose so,' Laura answered. 'I declare, it seems the winter's hardly begun, and now it's gone.'

'Yes, if this warm spell lasts the snow will be almost gone tomorrow,' Mary said. That meant that there would be no more sleigh rides.

'It's nice on the claim,' Laura said. She thought of the new calves and the baby chicks, and the garden growing, of lettuce and radishes and spring onions, and violets and the wild roses in June, and of Mary's coming home from college.

With Carrie she crossed the slushy street and went into the house. Both Pa and Ma were in the sitting room, and there in Mary's rocking chair sat a stranger. As Laura and Carrie stood hesitating near the door, he rose from his seat and smiled at them.

'Don't you know me, Laura?' he asked.

Then Laura did know him. She remembered his smile, so like Ma's.

'Oh, Uncle Tom! It's Uncle Tom!' she cried.

Pa laughed. 'I told you she'd know you, Tom.' And Ma smiled, so like his smile, while he shook hands with Laura and Carrie.

Carrie did not remember him; she had been only a baby in the Big Woods of Wisconsin. But Laura had been five years old when they went to the sugaring-off dance at Grandma's, and Uncle Tom had been there. He had been so quiet that she had hardly thought of him since then, but now she remembered the news that Aunt Docia had told of him when she stopped at the house by Plum Creek in Minnesota.

He was a small, quiet man with a gentle smile. Looking at him across the supper table, Laura could hardly believe that for years he had been a foreman of logging crews, taking the log drives out of the Big Woods and down the rivers. Although he was so small and soft-spoken, he had bossed the rough men and handled the dangerous log drives fearlessly. Laura remembered Aunt Docia's telling how he plunged in among the floating logs of a drive and, clinging to them, had dragged an injured man from the river to safety; this, though he could not swim.

Now he had much to tell Pa and Ma and Laura. He told of his wife Aunt Lily and their baby Helen. He told of Uncle Henry's family, Aunt Polly, Charley, and Albert.

After they left Silver Lake they had not gone to Montana, after all. They had stopped in the Black Hills. They were all there yet, except Cousin Louisa. She had married and gone on to Montana. As for Aunt Eliza and Uncle Peter, they were still living in eastern Minnesota, but Alice and Ella and Cousin Peter were somewhere in Dakota territory.

Carrie and Grace listened wide-eyed. Carrie remembered nothing of all these people, and Grace had never seen the Big Woods, nor a sugaring-off dance, nor known the Christmases when Uncle Peter and Aunt Eliza came visiting with the cousins Alice and Ella and Peter. Laura felt sorry for her little sister who had missed so much.

Suppertime passed quickly, and when the evening lamp was lighted and the family gathered around Uncle Tom in the sitting room, Pa still kept him speaking of the lumber camps and log drives, of roaring rivers and the wild, burly men of the logging camps. He told of them mildly, speaking in a voice as soft as Ma's, and smiling her gentle smile.

Pa said to him, 'So this is your first trip West,' and Uncle Tom answered quietly, 'Oh, no. I was with the first white men that ever laid eyes on the Black Hills.'

Pa and Ma were struck dumb for a moment. Then Ma asked, 'Whatever were you doing there, Tom?'

'Looking for gold,' said Uncle Tom.

'Too bad you didn't find a few gold mines,' Pa joked.

'Oh, we did,' Uncle Tom said. 'Only it didn't do us any good.'

'Mercy on us!' Ma softly exclaimed. 'Do tell us all about it.'

'Well, let's see. We started out from Sioux City, eight years ago,' Uncle Tom began. 'In October of '74. Twenty-six of us men, and one man brought along his wife and their nine-year-old boy.'

They travelled in covered wagons, with ox teams, and some saddle horses. Each man had a Winchester and small arms, and ammunition enough to last for eight months. They loaded supplies of flour, bacon, beans, and coffee into the wagons, and depended on hunting for most of their meat. Hunting was good; they got plenty of elk, antelope, and deer. The greatest trouble was lack of water on the open prairie. Luckily it was in early winter; there was plenty of snow, and they melted it at night to fill the water barrels.

The storms halted them some; during the blizzards they stayed in camp. Between storms the snow made hard going, and to lighten the loads they walked; even the woman walked a great part of the way. A good day's journey was fifteen miles.

So they pushed on into the unknown country, seeing nothing but the frozen prairie and the storms, and now and then a few Indians at a distance, till they came to a strange depression in the land. It barred their way, and stretched as far as they could see ahead and on both sides. It looked like an impossibility to get the wagons down into it, but there was nothing to do but cross it, so with considerable trouble they got the wagons down on to this sunken plain.

From the floor of it, strange formations of bare earth towered up all around them, hundreds of feet high. Their sides were steep, sometimes overhanging, cut and whittled by the winds that blew for ever. No vegetation grew on them, not a tree nor a bush nor a blade of grass. Their surface looked like dry caked mud, except in places where it was stained with different and brilliant colours. The floor of this sunken land was scattered thick with petrified shells and skulls and bones.

It was a heathenish place to be in, Uncle Tom said. The wagon wheels crunched over the bones, and those tall things seemed to turn as you went by, and some of them looked like faces, and outlandish idols. The wagons had to go between them, following the gulches or valleys. Winding around among those queer things, they got lost. It was three days before they could find their way out of that place, and it took a day's hard work to get the wagons up on its rim.

Looking back over it, an old prospector told Uncle Tom that it must be the Bad Lands of which he had heard tales from the Indians. And he added, 'I think that when God made the world He threw all the leftover waste into that hole.'

After that, they went on across the prairie until they came to the Black Hills. There they found shelter from the fierce prairie winds, but the going was hard because the valleys were full of snow and the hills were steep.

They had been travelling seventy-eight days when they made their last camp on French Creek. Here they cut pine logs from the hills, and built a stockade eighty feet square. They chopped the logs thirteen feet long, and set them upright, tightly together, sinking the bottom ends three feet into the ground. It was hard digging, the ground being frozen. On the inside of this wall, they battened it with smaller logs, pegged over every crack between the larger logs, with heavy wooden pegs.

At each corner of the square stockade they made stout log bastions, standing out, to give them a crossfire along the outside of the walls. In these bastions, and also along the walls, they cut portholes. The only entrance to this stockade was a double gate, twelve feet wide, made of large logs solidly pegged together with wooden pins. It was a good stockade, when they got it finished.

Inside it they built seven little log cabins, and there they lived through the winter. They hunted for their meat, and trapped for furs. The winter was bitter cold, but they pulled through, and towards spring they found gold, nuggets of it, and rich gold dust in the frozen gravel and under the ice in the creek beds. About the same time, the Indians attacked them. They could hold off the Indians all right, in that stockade. The trouble was that they would starve to death in it, if they could not get out of it to hunt. The Indians hung around, not fighting much but driving back any party that started out, and waiting for them to starve. So they cut down rations and tightened their belts, to hang on as long as they could before they had to kill their ox teams.

Then one morning they heard, far off, a bugle!

When Uncle Tom said that, Laura remembered the sound, long ago, echoing back from the Big Woods when Uncle George blew his army bugle. She cried out, 'Soldiers?'

'Yes,' Uncle Tom said. They knew they were all right now; the soldiers were coming. The lookouts yelled, and everybody crowded up into the bastions to watch. They heard the bugle again. Soon they heard the fife and drum, and then they saw the flag flying, and the troops coming behind it.

They threw open the gate and rushed out, all of them, fast as they could to meet the soldiers. The soldiers took them all prisoner, there where they were, and kept them there, while some of the troops went on and burned the

stockade, with everything in it. They burned the cabins and the wagons, and the furs, and killed the oxen.

'Oh, Tom!' Ma said as if she could not bear it.

'It was Indian country,' Uncle Tom said mildly. 'Strictly speaking, we had no right there.'

'Had you nothing at all to show for all that work and danger?' Ma mourned.

'Lost everything I started out with, but my rifle,' said Uncle Tom. 'The soldiers let us keep our guns. They marched us out on foot, prisoners.'

Pa was walking back and forth across the room. 'I'll be durned if I could have taken it!' he exclaimed. 'Not without some kind of scrap.'

'We couldn't fight the whole United States Army,' Uncle Tom said sensibly. 'But I did hate to see that stockade go up in smoke.'

'I know,' Ma said. 'To this day I think of the house we had to leave in Indian Territory. Just when Charles had got glass windows into it.'

Laura thought: 'All this happened to Uncle Tom while we were living on Plum Creek.' For some time no one spoke, then the old clock gave its warning wheeze and slowly and solemnly it struck, only once.

'My goodness! look at the time!' Ma exclaimed. 'I declare, Tom, you've held us spellbound. No wonder Grace is asleep. You girls hurry up to bed and take her with you, and Laura, you throw down the featherbed from my bed, and quilts, and I'll make a bed down here for Tom.'

'Don't rob your bed, Caroline,' Uncle Tom protested. 'I can sleep on the floor with a blanket, I've done so, often enough.'

'I guess Charles and I can sleep on a straw-tick for once,' said Ma. 'When I think how you slept cold and uncomfortable, so many nights on that trip.'

The cold winter of Uncle Tom's story was still in Laura's mind so strongly that next morning it was strange to hear the chinook softly blowing and the eaves dripping, and know that it was springtime and she was in the pleasant town. All day while she was sewing with Mrs McKee, Pa and Ma were visiting with Uncle Tom, and next day only Laura and Carrie and Grace went to Sunday School and church. Pa and Ma stayed at home in order not to waste a moment of Uncle Tom's short visit. He was leaving early

Monday morning for his home in Wisconsin.

Only scattered patches of snow were left on the muddy ground. There would be no more sleighing parties, Laura knew, and she was sorry.

Pa and Ma and Uncle Tom were talking of people she did not know, while they all sat around the table after a late Sunday dinner, when a shadow passed the window. Laura knew the knock at the door, and she hastened to open it, wondering why Almanzo had come.

'Would you like to go for the first buggy ride of spring?' he asked. 'With Cap and Mary Power and me?'

'Oh, yes!' she answered. 'Won't you come in, while I put on my hat and coat?'

'No, thank you,' he said, 'I'll wait outside.'

When she went out she saw that Mary and Cap were sitting in the back of Cap's two-seated buggy. Almanzo helped her up to the front seat and took the reins from Cap as he sat down beside her. Then Prince and Lady trotted away up the street and out on the prairie road towards the east.

No one else was out driving, so this was not a party, but Laura and Mary and Cap were laughing and merry. The road was slushy. Water and bits of snow spattered the horses and buggy and the linen lap robes across their knees. But the spring wind was soft on their faces and the sun was warmly shining.

Almanzo did not join in the merry talk. He drove

steadily, without a smile or a word, until Laura asked him what was the matter.

'Nothing,' he said; then he asked quickly, 'Who is that young man?'

No one was in sight anywhere. Laura exclaimed, 'What young man?'

'That you were talking with, when I came,' he said.

Laura was astonished. Mary burst out laughing. 'Now don't be jealous of Laura's uncle!' she said.

'Oh, did you mean him? That was Uncle Tom, Ma's brother,' Laura explained. Mary Power was still laughing so hard that Laura turned, just in time to see Cap snatch a hairpin from Mary's knot of hair.

'Suppose you pay some attention to me,' Cap said to Mary.

'Oh, stop it, Cap! Let me have it,' Mary cried, trying to seize the hairpin that Cap held out of her reach, while he snatched another one.

'Don't, Cap! Don't!' Mary begged, putting both hands over the knot of hair at the back of her neck. 'Laura, help me!'

Laura saw how desperate the situation was, for she alone knew that Mary wore a switch. Cap must be stopped, for if Mary lost any more hairpins, her beautiful large knot of hair would come off.

Just at that instant, a bit of snow flung from Prince's foot fell into Laura's lap. Cap's shoulder was turned to her as he struggled with Mary. Laura nipped up the bit of snow and neatly dropped it inside his collar at the back of his neck.

'Ow!' he yelled. 'Looks like you'd help a fellow, Wilder. Two girls against me is too many.'

'I'm busy driving,' Almanzo answered, and they all shouted with laughter. It was so easy to laugh in the springtime.

14

Holding Down a Claim

Uncle Tom went East on the train next morning. When Laura came home from school at noon, he was gone.

'No sooner had he gone,' said Ma, 'than Mrs McKee came. She is in distress, Laura, and she asked me if you would help her out.'

'Why, of course I will, if I can,' Laura said. 'What is it?'

Ma said that, hard as Mrs McKee had worked at dressmaking all that winter, the McKees could not afford to move to their claim yet. Mr McKee must keep his job at the lumberyard until they saved money enough to buy tools and seed and stock. He wanted Mrs McKee to take their little girl, Mattie, and live on the claim that summer, to hold it. Mrs McKee said she would not live out there on the prairie, all alone, with no one but Mattie; she said they could lose the claim, first.

'I don't know why she is so nervous about it,' said Ma. 'But it seems she is. It seems that being all alone, miles from anybody, scares her. So, as she told me, Mr McKee said he would let the claim go. After he went to work, she was thinking it over, and she came to tell me that if you would go with her, she would go hold down the claim. She said she would give you a dollar a week, just to stay with her as one of the family.'

'Where is the claim?' Pa inquired.

'It is some little distance north of Manchester,' said Ma. Manchester was a new little town, west of De Smet. 'Well, do you want to go, Laura?' Pa asked her.

'I guess so,' Laura said. 'I'll have to miss the rest of school, but I can make that up, and I'd like to go on earning something.'

'The McKees are nice folks, and it would be a real accommodation to them, so you may go if you want to,' Pa decided.

'It would be a pity, though, for you to miss Mary's visit home,' Ma worried.

'Maybe if I just get Mrs McKee settled on the claim and used to it, I could come home long enough to see Mary,' Laura pondered.

'Well, if you want to go, best go,' Ma said. 'We needn't cross a bridge till we come to it. Likely it will work out all right, somehow.'

So the next morning Laura rode with Mrs McKee and Mattie on the train to Manchester. She had been on the cars once before, when she came west from Plum Creek, so she felt like a seasoned traveller as she followed the brakeman with her satchel, down the aisle to a seat.

It was not as though she knew nothing about trains.

It was a seven-mile journey to Manchester. There the trainmen unloaded Mrs McKee's furniture from the boxcar in front of the passenger coach, and a teamster loaded it on to his wagon. Before he had finished, the hotelkeeper was banging his iron triangle with a spike, to call any strangers to dinner. So Mrs McKee and Laura and Mattie ate dinner in the hotel.

Soon afterwards the teamster drove the loaded wagon to the door, and helped them climb up to sit on the top of the load, among the rolls of bedding, the kitchen stove, the table and chairs and trunk and boxes of provisions. Mrs McKee rode in the seat with the teamster.

Sitting with their feet hanging down at the side of the wagon, Laura and Mattie clung to each other and to the ropes that bound the load to the wagon, as the team drew it bumping over the prairie. There was no road. The wagon wheels sank into the sod in places where it was soft from the melting snow, and the wagon and its load lurched from side to side. But it went very well until they came to a slough. Here, where the ground was lower, water stood in pools among the coarse slough grass.

'I don't know about this,' the teamster said, looking ahead. 'It looks pretty bad. But there's no way around; we'll just have to try it. Maybe we can go across so quick the wagon won't have time to sink down.'

As they came nearer to the slough, he said, 'Hang on, everybody!'

He picked up his whip and shouted to the horses. They went fast, and faster, till urged on by his shouts and the whip they broke into a run. Water rose up like wings from the plunging wagon wheels, while Laura hung on to the ropes and to Mattie with all her might.

Then all was quiet. Safe on the other side of the slough, the teamster stopped the horses to rest.

'Well, we made it!' he said. 'The wheels just didn't stay in one place long enough to settle through the sod. If a fellow got stuck in there, he'd be stuck for keeps.'

It was no wonder that he seemed relieved, for as Laura looked back across the slough she could see no wagon tracks. They were covered with water.

Driving on across the prairie, they came finally to a little new claim shanty, standing alone. About a mile away to the west was another, and far away to the east they could barely see a third.

'This is the place, ma'am,' the teamster said. 'I'll unload, and then haul you a jag of hay to burn, from that place a mile west. Fellow that had it last summer quit and went back East, but I see he left some haystacks there.'

He unloaded the wagon into the shanty, and set up the cookstove. Then he drove away to get the hay.

A partition cut the shanty into two tiny rooms. Mrs McKee and Laura set up a bedstead in the room with the cook-stove, and another in the other room. With the table, four small wooden chairs, and the trunk, they filled the little house.

'I'm glad I didn't bring anything more,' said Mrs McKee.

'Yes, as Ma would say, enough is as good as a feast,' Laura agreed.

The teamster came with a load of hay, then drove away towards Manchester. Now there were the two straw-ticks to fill with hay, the beds to make, and dishes to be unpacked. Then Laura twisted hay into sticks, from the little stack behind the shanty, and Mattie carried it in to keep the fire going while Mrs McKee cooked supper. Mrs McKee did not know how to twist hay, but Laura had learned during the Hard Winter.

As twilight came over the prairie, coyotes began to howl and Mrs McKee locked the door and saw that the windows were fastened.

'I don't know why the law makes us do this,' she said. 'What earthly good is it, to make a woman stay on a claim all summer?'

'It's a bet, Pa says,' Laura answered. 'The government bets a man a quarter-section of land, that he can't stay on it five years without starving to death.'

'Nobody could,' said Mrs McKee. 'Whoever makes these laws ought to know that a man that's got enough money to farm, has got enough to buy a farm. If he hasn't got money, he's got to earn it, so why do they make a law that he's got to stay on a claim, when he can't? All it means is, his wife and family have got to sit idle on it, seven months of the year. I could be earning something, dressmaking, to help buy tools and seeds, if somebody didn't have to sit on this claim. I declare to goodness, I don't know but sometimes I believe in women's rights. If women were voting and making laws, I believe they'd have better sense. Is that wolves?'

'No,' Laura said, 'It's only coyotes, they won't hurt anybody.'

They were all so tired that they did not light the lamp, but went to bed, Laura and Mattie in the kitchen and Mrs McKee in the front room. When everyone was quiet, the loneliness seemed to come into the shanty. Laura was not afraid, but never before had she been in such a lonely place without Pa and Ma and her sisters. The coyotes were far away, and farther. Then they were gone. The slough was so far away that the frogs could not be heard. There was no sound but the whispering of the prairie wind to break the silence.

The sun shining in Laura's face woke her to an empty day. The little work was soon done. There was nothing more to do, no books to study, no one to see. It was pleasant for a while. All that week Laura and Mrs McKee and Mattie did nothing but eat and sleep, and sit and talk or be silent. The sun rose and sank and the wind blew, and the prairie was empty of all but birds and cloud shadows.

Saturday afternoon they dressed for town and walked the two miles to Manchester to meet Mr McKee and walk home with him. He stayed until Sunday afternoon when they all walked to town again and Mr McKee took the train back to De Smet and his work. Then Mrs McKee and Laura and Mattie walked back to the claim for another week.

They were glad when Saturday came, but in a way it was a relief when Mr McKee was gone, for he was such a strict Presbyterian that on Sunday no one was allowed to laugh or even smile. They could only read the Bible and the catechism and talk gravely of religious subjects. Still, Laura liked him, for he was truly good and kind and never said a cross word.

This was the pattern of the weeks that passed, one after another, all alike, until April and May were gone.

The weather had grown warmer, and on the walks to town they heard the meadow larks singing beside the road where spring flowers bloomed. One warm Sunday afternoon the walk back from Manchester seemed longer than usual and tiring, and as they lagged a little along the way Mrs McKee said, 'It would be pleasanter for you to be riding in Wilder's buggy.'

'I likely won't do that any more,' Laura remarked. 'Someone else will be in my place before I go back.' She thought of Nellie Oleson. The Olesons' claim, she knew, was not far from Almanzo's.

'Don't worry,' Mrs McKee told her. 'An old bachelor doesn't pay so much attention to a girl unless he's serious. You will marry him yet.'

'Oh, no!' Laura said. 'No, indeed I won't! I wouldn't leave home to marry anybody.'

Then suddenly she realized that she was homesick. She wanted to be at home again so badly that she could hardly bear it. All that week she fought against her longing, hiding it from Mrs McKee, and on Saturday when they walked again to Manchester there was a letter waiting for her.

Ma had written that Mary was coming home, and Laura must come if Mrs McKee could find anyone else to stay with her. Ma hoped she could do so, for Laura must be at home when Mary was there.

She dreaded to speak of it to Mrs McKee, so she said nothing until at the supper table Mrs McKee asked what was troubling her. Then Laura told what Ma had written.

'Why, of course you must go home,' Mr McKee said at once. 'I will find someone to stay here.'

Mrs McKee was quiet for a time before she said, 'I don't want anyone but Laura to live with us. I would rather stay by ourselves. We are used to the place now, and nothing ever happens. Laura shall go home and Mattie and I will be all right alone.'

So Mr McKee carried Laura's satchel on the Sunday afternoon walk to Manchester, and she said good-bye to

Mrs McKee and Mattie and got on the train with him, going home.

All the way she thought of them, standing lonely at the station, and walking the two miles back to the lonely shanty where they must stay, doing nothing but eating and sleeping and listening to the wind, for five months more. It was a hard way to earn a homestead, but there was no other way, for that was the law.

15

Mary Comes Home

Laura was so glad to be at home again, out on Pa's claim. It was good to milk the cow, and to drink all she wanted of milk, and to spread butter on her bread, and eat again of Ma's good cottage cheese. There were lettuce leaves to be picked in the garden, too, and little red radishes. She had not realized that she was so hungry for these good things to eat. Mrs McKee and Mattie could not get them, of course, while they were holding down their claim.

At home now there were eggs, too, for Ma's flock was doing well. Laura helped Carrie hunt for nests that the hens hid in the hay at the stable and in the tall grass nearby.

Grace found a nest of kittens hidden in the manger. They were grandchildren of the little kitten that Pa had bought for fifty cents, and Kitty felt her responsibility. She thought that she should hunt for them as well as for her own kittens. She brought in more gophers than all of them could eat, and every day she piled the extra ones by the house door for Ma.

'I declare,' Ma said, 'I never was so embarrassed by a cat's generosity.'

The day came when Mary was coming home. Pa and Ma drove to town to fetch her, and even the train seemed special that afternoon as it came at last, unrolling its black smoke into a melting line low on the sky. From the rise of ground behind the stable and the garden, they saw the white steam puff up from its engine and heard its whistle; its far rumbling was still, and they knew that it had stopped in town and that Mary must be there now.

What excitement there was when at last the wagon came up from the slough, with Mary sitting on the seat between Pa and Ma. Laura and Carrie both talked at once and Mary tried to talk to both at the same time. Grace was in everyone's way, her hair flying and her blue eyes wide. Kitty went out through the doorway like a streak, with her tail swelled to a big brush. Kitty did not like strangers, and she had forgotten Mary.

'Weren't you afraid to come all by yourself on the cars?' Carrie asked.

'Oh, no,' Mary smiled. 'I had no trouble. We learn to do things by ourselves, at college. It is part of our education.'

She did seem much more sure of herself, and she moved easily around the house, instead of sitting quiet in her chair. Pa brought in her trunk, and she went to it, knelt down and unlocked and opened it quite as if she saw it. Then she took from it, one after another, the presents she had brought.

For Ma there was a lamp mat of woven braid, with a fringe all around it of many-coloured beads strung on stout thread.

'It is beautiful,' Ma said in delight.

Laura's gift was a bracelet of blue and white beads strung on thread and woven together, and Carrie's was a ring of pink and white beads interwoven.

'Oh, how pretty! how pretty!' Carrie exclaimed. 'And it fits, too; it fits perfectly!'

For Grace there was a little doll's chair, of red and green beads strung on wire. Grace was so overcome as she took it carefully into her hands that she could hardly say thank you to Mary.

'This is for you, Pa,' Mary said, as she gave him a blue silk handkerchief. 'I didn't make this, but I chose it myself. Blanche and I . . . Blanche is my roommate. We went downtown to find something for you. She can see colours if they are bright, but the clerk didn't know it. We thought it would be fun to mystify him, so Blanche signalled the colours to me, and he thought we could tell them by touch. I knew by the feeling that it was good silk. My, we did fool that clerk!' and, remembering, Mary laughed.

Mary had often smiled, but it was a long time since they had heard her laugh out, as she used to when she was

a little girl. All that it had cost to send Mary to college was more than repaid by seeing her so gay and confident.

'I'll bet this was the prettiest handkerchief in Vinton, Iowa!' Pa said.

'I don't see how you put the right colours into your beadwork,' Laura said, turning the bracelet on her wrist. 'Every little bead in this lovely bracelet is right. You can't do that by fooling a clerk.'

'Some seeing person puts the different colours in

separate boxes,' Mary explained. 'Then we only have to remember where they are.'

'You can do that easily,' Laura agreed. 'You always could remember things. You know I never could say as many Bible verses as you.'

'It surprises my Sunday School teacher now, how many of them I know,' said Mary. 'Knowing them was a great help to me, Ma. I could read them so easily with my fingers in raised print and in Braille, that I learned how to read everything sooner than anyone else in my class.'

'I am glad to know that, Mary,' was all that Ma said, and her smile trembled, but she looked happier than when Mary had given her the beautiful lamp mat.

'Here is my Braille slate,' said Mary, lifting it from her trunk. It was an oblong of thin steel in a frame, as large as a school slate, with a narrow steel band across it. The band was cut into several rows of open squares, and it would slide up and down, or could be fastened in place at any point. Tied to the frame by a string was a pencil-shaped piece of steel that Mary said was a stylus.

'How do you use it?' Pa wanted to know.

'Watch and I'll show you,' said Mary.

They all watched while she laid a sheet of thick, cream-coloured paper on the slate, under the slide. She moved the slide to the top of the frame and secured it there. Then with the point of the stylus she pressed, rapidly, here and there in the corners of the open squares.

'There,' she said, slipping the paper out and turning it over. Wherever the stylus had pressed, there was a tiny bump, that could easily be felt with the fingers. The bumps made different patterns, the size of the squares, and these were the Braille letters.

'I am writing to Blanche to tell her that I am safely home,' said Mary. 'I must write to my teacher, too.' She turned the paper over, put it in the frame again, and slipped the slide down, ready to go on writing on the blank space. 'I will finish them later.'

'It is wonderful that you can write to your friends and they can read your letters,' said Ma. 'I can hardly believe that you are really getting the college education that we always wanted you to have.'

Laura was so happy that she felt like crying, too.

'Well, well,' Pa broke in. 'Here we stand talking, when Mary must be hungry and it's chore time. Let's do our work now, and we will have longer to talk afterwards.'

'You are right, Charles,' Ma quickly agreed. 'Supper will be ready by the time you are ready for it.'

While Pa took care of the horses, Laura hurried to do the milking, and Carrie make a quick fire to bake the dough that Ma was mixing.

Supper was ready when Pa came from the stable and Laura had strained the milk.

It was a happy family, all together again, as they ate of the browned hashed potatoes, poached fresh eggs, and delicious bread with Ma's good butter. Pa and Ma drank their fragrant tea, but Mary drank milk with the other girls. 'It is a treat,' she said. 'We don't have such good milk at college.'

There was so much to ask and tell that almost nothing was fully said, but tomorrow would be another long day with Mary. And it was like old times again, when Laura and Mary went to sleep as they used to in their bed where Laura for so long had been sleeping alone.

'It's warm weather,' Mary said, 'so I won't be putting my cold feet on you as I used to do.'

'I'm so glad you're here that I wouldn't complain,' Laura answered. 'It would be a pleasure.'

16

Summer Days

It was such a joy to have Mary at home that the summer days were not long enough for all their pleasures. Listening to Mary's stories of her life in college, reading aloud to her, planning and sewing to put her clothes in order, and once more going with her for long walks in the late afternoon, made the time go by too swiftly.

One Saturday morning Laura went to town to match Mary's last winter's best dress in silk, to make a new collar and cuffs. She found just what she wanted in a new milliner's and dressmaker's shop, and while Miss Bell was wrapping the little package she said to Laura, 'I hear you're a good sewer. I wish you would come and help me. I'll pay you fifty cents a day, from seven o'clock to five, if you'll bring your dinner.'

Laura looked around the pleasant, new place, with the pretty hats in two windows, bolts of ribbon in a glass showcase, and silks and velvets on the shelves behind it. There was a sewing machine, with an unfinished dress lying across it, and another lay on a chair nearby.

'You can see there is more work here than I can do,'

Miss Bell said in her quiet voice. Miss Bell was a young woman and Laura thought her handsome with her tall figure and dark hair and eyes.

Laura decided that it would be pleasant to work with her.

'I will come if Ma is willing I should,' she promised.

'Come Monday morning if you can,' said Miss Bell.

Laura left the shop and went up the street to the post office to mail a letter for Mary. There she met Mary Power, who was on her way to do an errand at the lumberyard. They had not seen each other since the buggy ride in early spring, and there was so much to talk about that Mary begged Laura to come with her.

'All right, I will,' said Laura. 'I'd like to ask Mr McKee how Mrs McKee and Mattie are getting along, anyway.'

They walked slowly, talking all the way up the street, across the cindery railroad tracks and the dusty street to the corner of the lumberyard, and there they stood talking.

A yoke of oxen was coming slowly into town on the country road from the north, hauling a lumber wagon. A man walked beside the farther ox, and Laura idly watched him as he swung a long whip. The oxen trudged along until nearly to the corner, then started ahead quickly.

Laura and Mary stepped back. The man commanded, 'Whoa! Haw!' But the oxen did not turn left. They swung to the right, around the corner.

'Gee, then! Go where you've a mind to!' the driver

ordered them, impatiently, but joking. Then he looked at the girls, and they exclaimed together, 'Almanzo Wilder!'

He raised his hat with a cheerful flourish to them, and hurried along the street with the oxen.

'I didn't know him without his horses!' Laura laughed.

'And the way he was dressed,' Mary disparaged him. 'In those rough clothes and ugly heavy shoes.'

'He is likely breaking sod, and that is why he had oxen. He wouldn't work Prince and Lady so hard,' Laura explained, more to herself than to Mary Power.

'Everybody is working,' Mary remarked. 'Nobody can have fun in the summertime. But Nellie Oleson is going to ride behind those horses yet, if she possibly can. You know the Olesons' claim is a little way east of the Wilder boys' claims.'

'Have you seen her lately?' Laura asked.

'I never see anybody,' Mary answered. 'All the girls are out on their fathers' claims, and Cap is teaming every day. Ben Woodsworth is working at the depot, and nobody can get a word with Frank Harthorn nowadays, he works all the time in the store since his father has made him a partner. Minnie and Arthur are out with their folks on their homestead, and here I haven't seen you since early April.'

'Never mind, we'll see each other all next winter. Besides, I am coming to town to work if Ma says I may,' and Laura told Mary that she expected to sew for Miss Bell.

Suddenly she saw that the sun was almost overhead. She stopped only a moment in the lumberyard office, to hear from Mr McKee that Mrs McKee and Mattie were getting along all right, though they still missed her. Then quickly she said goodbye to Mary and hurried away on her walk home. She had stayed in town too long. Though she walked so fast that she was almost running, dinner was ready when she reached home.

'I am sorry I stayed so long, but so many things happened,' she made excuse.

'Yes?' Ma inquired, and Carrie asked, 'What happened?'

Laura told of meeting Mary Power and of seeing Mr McKee. 'I stayed too long with Mary Power,' she confessed. 'The time went so quickly that I did not know it was so late.' Then she told the rest. 'Miss Bell wants me to work for her in her shop. May I, Ma?'

'Why, Laura, I declare I don't know,' Ma exclaimed. 'You have only just got home.'

'She will pay me fifty cents a day, from seven o'clock to five, if I bring my own dinner,' Laura told them.

'That is fair enough,' said Pa. 'You take your own dinner, but you get off an hour early.'

'But you came home to be with Mary,' Ma objected.

'I know, Ma, but I will see her every night and morning and all day Sunday,' Laura argued. 'I don't know why, but I feel I ought to be earning something.'

'That is the way it is, once you begin to earn,' Pa said.

'I will be earning three dollars a week,' said Laura. 'And seeing Mary, too. We will have lots of time to do things together, won't we, Mary?'

'Yes, and I will do all your housework while you're gone,' Mary offered. 'Then on Sundays we'll have our walks.'

'That reminds me, the new church is done,' said Pa. 'We must all go to church tomorrow morning.'

'I'll be so glad to see the new church! I can hardly believe there is one!' Mary said.

'It's there sure enough,' Pa assured her. 'We'll see for ourselves tomorrow.'

'And the next day?' Laura asked.

'Yes, you may go to work for Miss Bell. You can try it for a while anyway,' Ma said.

Sunday morning Pa hitched the horses to the wagon, and they all rode to church. It was large and new, with long seats that were comfortable to sit in. Mary liked it very much, after the small chapel at college, but she knew hardly anyone there. On the way home she said, 'There were so many strangers.'

'They come and they go,' Pa told her. 'No sooner do I get acquainted with a newcomer than he sells the relinquishment of his claim and goes on West, or else his family can't stand it here and he sells out and moves back East. The few that stick are so busy that we don't have time to know each other.'

'It doesn't matter,' Mary said. 'I will soon be going

back to college, and I know everyone there.'

After the Sunday dinner, when the work was done, Carrie sat down to read the *Youth's Companion*, Grace went to play with the kittens in the clean grass near the door, Ma rested in her rocking chair by the open window, and Pa lay down for his Sunday nap. Then Laura said, 'Come, Mary, let's go for our walk.'

They walked across the prairie to the south, and all along their way the wild June roses were blooming. Laura gathered them until she filled Mary's arm with all she could hold.

'Oh, how sweet!' Mary kept saying. 'I have missed the spring violets, but nothing is sweeter than prairie roses. It is so good to be home again, Laura. Even if I can't stay long.'

'We have until the middle of August,' said Laura. 'But the roses won't last that long.'

'"Gather ye rosebuds while ye may,"' Mary began, and she quoted the poem for Laura. Then as they walked on together in the rose-scented warm wind, she talked of her studies in literature. 'I am planning to write a book some day,' she confided. Then she laughed. 'But I planned to teach school, and you are doing that for me, so maybe you will write the book.'

'I, write a book?' Laura hooted. She said blithely, 'I'm going to be an old maid schoolteacher, like Miss Wilder. Write your own book! What are you going to write about?'

But Mary was diverted from the subject of books. She inquired, 'Where is that Wilder boy, that Ma wrote me about? It seems like he'd be around sometime.'

'I think he is too busy on his claim. Everybody is busy,' Laura answered. She did not mention seeing him in town. For some reason that she could not explain, she felt shy of talking about it. She and Mary turned and went rather quietly back to the house, bringing into it the fragrance of the roses they carried.

Swiftly that summer went by. Every weekday Laura walked to town in the early morning, carrying her lunch pail. Often Pa walked with her, for he was doing carpenter work on new buildings that newcomers were building. Laura could hear the hammers and saws while she sewed steadily all day long, pausing only to eat her cold lunch at noon. Then, often with Pa, she walked home again. Sometimes there was a pain between her shoulders from bending over her work, but that always disappeared during the walk, and then came the happy evening at home.

At supper she told of all she had seen and heard in Miss Bell's shop, Pa told any news he had gathered, and they all talked of the happenings on the claim and in the house: how the crops were growing, how Ma was getting along with Mary's sewing, how many eggs Grace had found, and that the old speckled hen had stolen her nest and just come off with twenty chicks.

It was at the supper table that Ma reminded them that tomorrow was Fourth of July. 'What are we going to do about it?'

'I don't see that we can do anything, Caroline. No way that I know of, to prevent tomorrow's being the Fourth,' Pa teased.

'Now, Charles,' Ma reproached him, smiling. 'Are we going to the celebration?'

There was silence around the table.

'I cannot hear you when you all talk at once,' Ma teased in her turn. 'If we are going, we must think about it tonight. I've been so enjoying having Mary here that I forgot about the Fourth, and nothing is prepared for a celebration.'

'My whole vacation is a celebration, and it seems to me enough,' Mary said quietly.

'I have been in town every day. It would be a treat to me to miss a day.' Then Laura added, 'But there are Carrie and Grace.'

Pa laid down his knife and fork. 'I'll tell you what. Caroline, you and the girls cook a good dinner, I will go to town in the morning and get some candy and firecrackers. We will have our own Fourth of July celebration right here at home. What do you say to that?'

'Get lots of candy, Pa!' Grace begged, while Carrie urged, 'And lots of firecrackers!'

Everyone had such a good time next day that they all

agreed it was much more fun than going to town. Once or twice Laura wondered if Almanzo Wilder were in town with the brown horses, and the thought of Nellie Oleson just crossed her mind. But if Almanzo wanted to see her again, he knew where she was. It was not her place to do anything about it, and she didn't intend to.

All too soon the summer was gone. In the last week of August Mary went back to college, leaving an emptiness in the house. Now Pa cut the oats and wheat with his old hand cradle, because the fields were still so small that they would not pay for having a harvester. When the corn was ripe he cut it and shocked it in the field. He was thin and tired from all the hard work he had done, in town and in the fields, and he was restless because people were settling the country so thickly.

I would like to go West,' he told Ma one day. 'A fellow doesn't have room to breathe here any more.'

'Oh, Charles! No room, with all this great prairie around you?' Ma said. 'I was so tired of being dragged from pillar to post, and I thought we were settled here.'

'Well, I guess we are, Caroline. Don't fret. It's just that my wandering foot gets to itching, I guess. Anyway I haven't won that bet with Uncle Sam yet, and we stay right here till we win it! till I can prove up on this homestead claim.'

Laura knew how he felt for she saw the look in his blue eyes as he gazed over the rolling prairie westward from the open door where he stood. He must stay in a settled country for the sake of them all, just as she must teach school again, though she did so hate to be shut into a schoolroom.

17

Breaking the Colts

October days had come, and the wild geese were flying south, when once more Pa loaded the furniture on the wagon and they all moved back to town. Other people were moving in from the country, and the seats in the schoolhouse were filling up.

Most of the big boys were not coming to school any more. Some had moved to the claims to stay. Ben Woodworth was working in the depot, Frank Harthorn was busy in the store, and Cap Garland was working with his team, hauling hay and coal or anything he was hired to move in town or country. Still there were not seats enough in the schoolhouse, for the country was full of newcomers whose children came to school. The smaller pupils were crowded three in a seat, and it was certain now that a larger schoolhouse must be built before next winter.

One day when Laura and Carrie came from school, they found company sitting with Ma in the front room. The man was a stranger, but Laura felt that she should know the young woman who looked at her soberly. Ma was smiling; she said nothing for a moment, while Laura and the woman looked at each other.

Then the woman smiled, and Laura knew her. She was Cousin Alice! Alice, who with Ella and Peter had come to spend Christmas in the log house in the Big Woods. Alice and Mary had been the big girls then; Ella had been Laura's playmate. Now while Laura greeted Alice with a kiss, she asked, 'Did Ella come, too?'

'No, she and her husband couldn't come,' Alice said. 'But here is a cousin you haven't met yet, my husband, Arthur Whiting.'

Arthur was tall, with dark hair and eyes; he was pleasant and Laura liked him, but though he and Alice stayed a week, he always seemed to be a stranger. Alice was so much like Mary that she belonged in the family, and Laura

and Carrie hurried home from school because Alice would be sitting in the sunny front room with Ma.

In the evenings they all popped corn and made toffee, listened to Pa's fiddle, and endlessly talked of old times and of plans for the future.

Arthur's brother, Lee, was Ella's husband, and they had taken adjoining claims only forty miles away. Peter was coming out in the spring.

'It has been such a long time since we were together in the Big Woods, and now we are gathering out here on the prairie,' Alice said one evening.

'If only your mother and father would come,' Ma said wistfully.

'I think they will stay in eastern Minnesota,' Alice told her. 'They only came that far, and there they seem contented.'

'It's a queer thing,' said Pa. 'People always moving west. Out here it is like the edge of a wave, when a river's rising. They come and they go, back and forth, but all the time the bulk of them keep moving on west.'

Alice and Arthur stayed only a week. Early Saturday morning, well wrapped up, with heated flatirons at their feet and hot baked potatoes in their pockets, they set out on their forty-mile sleigh ride home. 'Give my love to Ella,' Laura said, as she kissed Alice again for good-bye.

It was wonderful sleighing weather, clear and colder than zero, with deep snow and no sign of a blizzard cloud.

But this winter there were no more sleighing parties. Perhaps the boys were working their horses too hard all the week. Now and then Laura saw Almanzo and Cap at a distance; they were breaking a pair of colts to drive and seemed to be having a busy time.

On Sunday afternoon Laura saw them passing several times. Sometimes Almanzo, and sometimes Cap, was braced in the cutter, holding with all his might to the reins, while the wild colts tried to break away and run. Pa looked up from his paper once and said, 'One of those young fellows will break his neck yet. There's not a man in town would tackle handling that team.'

Laura was writing a letter to Mary. She paused and thought how fortunate it was that during the Hard Winter Almanzo and Cap had taken chances no one else would take, when they had gone after wheat for the starving people.

She had finished her letter and folded it, when someone knocked at the door. Laura opened it, and Cap Garland stood there. With his flashing grin that lighted his whole face, he asked, 'Would you like a sleigh ride behind the colts?'

Laura's heart sank. She liked Cap, but she did not want him to ask her to go sleigh riding, and all in an instant she thought of Mary Power and of Almanzo and she did not know what to say.

But Cap went on speaking. 'Wilder asked me to ask

you, because the colts won't stand. He'll be by here in a minute and pick you up, if you'd like to go.'

'Yes, I would!' Laura exclaimed. 'I'll be ready. Come in?'

'No thanks, I'll tell him,' Cap replied.

Laura hurried, but the colts were pawing and prancing impatiently when she came. Almanzo was holding them with both hands, and said to her, 'Sorry I can't help you,' as she got herself into the cutter. As soon as she was seated, they dashed away down the street.

No one else was out driving, so the street was clear as the colts fought to break away from Almanzo's grip on the lines. Far out on the road south of town they went racing.

Laura sat quietly watching their flying feet and laid-back ears. This was fun. It reminded her of a time long ago when she and Cousin Lena let the black ponies run away across the prairie. The wind blew hard and cold on her face, and bits of snow pelted back on to the robes. Then the colts tossed their heads, pricked up their ears, and let Almanzo turn their frisky steps back towards town.

He looked at her curiously. 'Do you know there isn't a man in town except Cap Garland who will ride behind these colts?' he asked.

'Pa said so,' Laura replied.

'Then why did you come?' Almanzo wanted to know.

'Why, I thought you could drive them,' Laura said in surprise, and asked in her turn, 'But why don't you drive Prince and Lady?'

'I want to sell these colts, and they've got to be broken to drive first,' Almanzo explained.

Laura said no more as the colts tried again to run. They were headed towards home and wanted to get there quickly. It took all Almanzo's attention and muscle to hold them to a fast and fighting trot. Main Street flashed by in a blur, and far out on the prairie to the north Almanzo quieted the colts and turned them again. Then Laura laughed, 'If this is breaking them, I'm glad to help!'

They said little more until an hour had gone by and the winter sun was sinking. Then as Almanzo held the colts and Laura quickly slipped out of the cutter at Pa's door, he said, 'I'll come for you Sunday.' The colts jumped and dashed away before Laura could reply.

'I am afraid to have you ride behind those horses,' Ma said as Laura came in.

Pa looked up from his paper. 'Does seem like Wilder is trying to get you killed. But I'd say you are enjoying it from the way your eyes are shining,' he added.

After this, Almanzo came on Sunday afternoons to take Laura for a sleigh ride. But he and Cap always drove the colts first, more than half the afternoon, to quiet them, and nothing that Laura could say would persuade Almanzo to let her ride before the colts were somewhat tired.

There was a Christmas tree that year at the new church. Laura and Carrie remembered a Christmas tree long ago in Minnesota, but Grace had never seen one.

Laura thought the best part of that Christmas was seeing Grace's delighted face when she looked at the Christmas tree with its lighted candles shining, the bright-coloured mosquito-net bags of candy and the presents hanging from its branches.

But while she was waiting for Grace's Christmas doll to be brought to her from the tree, Laura was given a package which surprised her so much that she was sure there was some mistake. It was a small black leather case lined with blue silk. Against the lovely blue shone, all white, an ivory-backed hairbrush and comb. Laura looked again at the wrapping paper; her name was plainly written on it, in a handwriting she did not know.

'Whoever could have given me such a present, Ma?' she asked.

Then Pa leaned to admire it, too, and his eyes twinkled. 'I could not swear who gave it to you, Laura,' he said. 'But I can tell you one thing. I saw Almanzo Wilder buying that very case in Bradley's drugstore,' and he smiled at Laura's astonishment.

18

The Perry School

The first March winds were blowing hard the next Thursday when Laura came home from school. She was breathless, not only from struggling with the wind, but from the news she brought. Before she could tell it, Pa spoke.

'Could you be ready to move to the claim this week, Caroline?'

'This week,' said Ma in surprise.

'The school district's going to put up a schoolhouse on Perry's claim, just south of our south line,' Pa said. 'All the neighbours will help to build it, but they want to hire me to boss the job. We ought to be moved out before I begin, and if we go this week, there'll be plenty of time to finish the schoolhouse before the first of April.'

'We can go any day you say, Charles,' Ma answered.

'Day after tomorrow, then,' said Pa. 'And there is something else. Perry says their school board would like to have Laura teach the school. How about it, Laura? You will have to get a new certificate.'

'Oh, I would *like* to have a school so near home,' said Laura. Then she told her news. 'Teachers' examinations are tomorrow. Mr Owen announced them today. They will be held at the schoolhouse, so there's no school tomorrow. I do hope I can get a second-grade certificate.'

'I am sure you can,' Carrie encouraged her stoutly. 'You always know your lessons.'

Laura was a little doubtful. 'I have no time to review and study. If I pass, I have to do it on what I know now.'

'That is the best way, Laura,' Ma told her. 'If you tried to study in a hurry you would only be confused. If you get a second grade we will all be glad, and if it is only third grade we will be glad of that.'

'I will try my best,' was all that Laura could promise. Next morning she set out alone, and nervously, to the teachers' examinations at the schoolhouse. The room seemed strange, with only a few strangers sitting here and there among empty seats, and Mr Williams at the desk instead of Mr Owen.

The lists of questions were already written on the blackboard. All morning there was silence, except for the scratching of pens and small rustles of paper. Mr Williams gathered the papers at the end of every hour, whether they were finished or not, and graded them at his desk.

Laura finished each of her papers in good time, and that afternoon, with a smile, Mr Williams handed her a certificate. His smile told her, even before she quickly saw the words he had written on it, 'Second Grade.'

She walked home, but really she was dancing, running, laughing, and shouting with jubilation. Quietly she handed the certificate to Ma, and saw Ma's smile light her whole face.

'I told you so! I told you you would get it,' Carrie gloated.

'I was sure you would pass,' Ma praised her, 'if you didn't get bothered by your first public examination among strangers.'

'Now I will tell you the rest of the good news,' Pa smiled. 'I thought I'd save it as a reward, for after the examination. Perry says the school board will pay you twenty-five dollars a month for a three months' school, April, May, and June.'

Laura was nearly speechless. 'Oh!' she exclaimed. Then, 'I didn't expect . . . Why! Why, Pa . . . that will be a little more than a dollar a day.'

Grace's blue eyes were perfectly round. In solemn awe she said, 'Laura will be rich.'

They all burst out laughing so merrily that Grace had to join in, without knowing why. When they were sober again, Pa said, 'Now we'll move out to the claim and build that schoolhouse.'

So during the last weeks of March, Laura and Carrie walked to school again from the claim. The weather was spring-like in spite of March winds, and every evening when they came home they saw that more work had been done on the little schoolhouse that was rising from the prairie a little way to the south.

In the last days of March, the Perry boys painted it white. There never had been a prettier, small schoolhouse.

It stood snowy white on the green land, and its rows of windows shone brightly in the morning sunshine as Laura walked towards it across the short, new grass.

Little Clyde Perry, seven years old, was playing by the doorstep where his First Reader had been carefully laid. He put the key of the new door into Laura's hand and said solemnly, 'My father sent you this.'

Inside, too, the schoolhouse was bright and shining. The walls of new lumber were clean and smelled fresh. Sunshine streamed in from the eastern windows. Across the whole end of the room was a clean, new blackboard. Before it stood the teacher's desk, a boughten desk, smoothly varnished. It gleamed honey-coloured in the sunlight, and on its flat top lay a large Webster's Unabridged Dictionary.

Before this desk stood three rows of new, boughten seats. Their smooth honey-coloured finish matched the teacher's desk. The ends of the outside rows were tight against the walls; between them there was space for the third row and the two aisles. There were four seats in each row.

Laura stood a moment in the doorway, looking at that fresh, bright expensive room. Then going to her desk, she set her dinner pail on the floor beneath it and hung her sunbonnet on a nail in the wall.

A small clock stood ticking beside the big dictionary; its hands stood at nine o'clock. It must have been wound last night, Laura thought. Nothing could be more complete and perfect that this beautiful little schoolhouse.

She heard children's voices at the door, and she went to call her pupils in.

Besides Clyde, there were two others, a little boy and a girl who said their name was Johnson. They were both in the Second Reader. That was the size of the school. In all the term, no more children came.

Laura felt that she was not earning twenty-five dollars a month, teaching only three children. But when she said this at home, Pa replied that these three were as much entitled to schooling as if there were a dozen, and that she was entitled to pay for the time that she spent teaching them.

'But, Pa,' she protested. 'Twenty-five dollars a month!'

'Don't let that worry you,' he answered. 'They are glad to have you at that price. Large schools are paying thirty dollars.'

It must be right, since Pa said so. Laura contented herself by giving each little pupil the very best of schooling. They were all quick to learn. Besides reading and spelling, she taught them to write words and figures, and how to add and subtract. She was proud of their progress.

Never had she been so happy as she was that spring. In the fresh, sweet mornings she walked to her school, past the little hollow blue with violets that scented all the air. Her pupils were happy, too, every one as good as gold, and eager and quick to learn. They were as careful as she not to mar or dim the freshness of their shining new schoolhouse.

Laura took her own books to school, and while her little pupils studied at their desks, between questions, she studied at hers, with help from the big dictionary. At recess and during the long noon hour, she knitted lace while the children played. And always she was aware of the cloud shadows chasing each other outside the windows, where meadow larks sang and the little striped gophers ran swiftly about their affairs.

After each happy day, there was the walk home past the little hollow where the violets grew, spreading their fragrance on the air.

Sometimes on Saturday Laura walked westward across the prairie to Reverend Brown's house – on his claim. It was a long mile-and-a-half walk, and she and Ida always made it longer by going to the highest point of the rise of ground beyond the house. From there they could see the Wessington Hills, sixty miles away, looking like a blue cloud on the horizon.

'They are so beautiful that they make me want to go to them,' Laura said once.

'Oh, I don't know,' Ida replied. 'When you got there, they would be just hills, covered with ordinary buffalo grass like this,' and she kicked at a tuft of the grass where the green of spring was showing through last year's dead blades.

In a way, that was true; and in another way, it wasn't. Laura could not say what she meant, but to her the Wessington Hills were more than grassy hills. Their shadowy outlines drew her with the lure of far places. They were the essence of a dream.

Walking home in the late afternoon, Laura still thought of the Wessington Hills, how mysterious their vague shadow was against the blue sky, far away across miles after miles of green, rolling prairie. She wanted to travel on and on, over those miles, and see what lay beyond the hills.

That was the way Pa felt about the West, Laura knew. She knew, too, that like him she must be content to stay where she was, to help with the work at home and teach school.

That night Pa asked her what she planned to do with all her school money when she got it.

'Why,' Laura said, 'I'll give it to you and Ma.'

'I'll tell you what I have been thinking,' said Pa. 'We should have an organ when Mary comes home, so she can keep up the music she's learning in college, and it would be nice for you girls, too. Some folks in town are selling out and going back East, and they have an organ. I can get it for one hundred dollars. It is a good organ, I tried

154

it to see. If you will pay your school money for it, I can make up the other twenty-five dollars, and besides I can build another room on this house so we will have a place to put it.'

'I would be glad to help buy the organ,' Laura said. 'But you know I won't have the seventy-five dollars till after my school is out.'

'Laura,' Ma put in, 'You should think about getting yourself some clothes. Your calicoes are all right for school, but you need a new summer dress for best; your year before last's lawn is really past letting down any more.'

'I know, Ma, but think of having an organ,' said Laura. 'And I think I can work for Miss Bell again, and earn some clothes. The trouble is that I haven't got my school money yet.'

'You are certain to get it,' Pa said. 'Are you sure you want to buy an organ with it?'

'Oh, yes!' Laura told him. 'There's nothing I'd like more than to have an organ that Mary can play when she comes home.'

'Then that's settled!' Pa said happily. 'I'll pay down the twenty-five, and those folks'll trust me for the balance till you get it. By jinks! I feel like celebrating. Bring me my fiddle, Half-Pint, and we'll have a little music without the organ.'

While they all sat in the soft spring twilight, Pa played and sang merrily:

'Here's to the maiden of bashful fifteen,
Here's to the widow of fifty,
Here's to the flaunting extravagant quean,
And here's to the housewife that's thrifty!
Here's to the charmer whose dimples we
    prize,
Now to the maid who has none, sir!
Here's to the girl with a pair of blue eyes,
And here's to the nymph with but one, sir!'

His mood changed, and so did the fiddle's. They sang:

'Oh, I went down south for to see my Sal,
Sing polly-wolly-doodle all the way!
My Sally was a spunky gal,
Sing polly-wolly-doodle all the day.
Farewell, farewell, farewell my fairy fay,
I'm off to Louisiana
For to see my Susy Anna,
Singing polly-wolly-doodle all the day!'

The dusk was deepening. The land flattened to blackness and in the clear air above it the large stars hung low, while the fiddle sang a wandering song of its own.

Then Pa said, 'Here is one for you girls.' And softly he sang with the fiddle:

'Golden years are passing by,
Happy, happy golden years,
Passing on the wings of time,
These happy golden years.
Call them back as they go by,
Sweet their memories are,
Oh, improve them as they fly,
These happy golden years.'

Laura's heart ached as the music floated away and was
gone in the spring night under the stars.

19

The Brown Poplin

Now that Ma had spoken of her clothes, Laura saw that she should do something about them. So early Saturday morning she walked to town to see Miss Bell.

'Indeed I shall be glad to have your help,' said Miss Bell. 'I've been at my wit's end to keep up with all the work, there are so many new people in town. But I thought you were teaching school.'

'Not on Saturdays,' Laura laughed. 'Beginning in July, I can work all week if you like.'

So every Saturday she sewed all day long for Miss Bell. Before her school ended, she was able to buy ten yards of a beautiful brown poplin which Miss Bell had ordered from Chicago. And every evening when she went home there was something new to see, for Ma was making up the brown poplin for her, and Pa was building the new room for the organ.

He built it across the east end of the house, with a door in the north looking towards town, and windows in both the east and the south walls. Under the southern window he built a low seat, wide enough for one person

158

to sleep on, so that it could be used as an extra bed.

One evening when Laura came home, the new room was complete. Pa had brought the organ; it stood against the north wall by the door. It was a beautiful organ, of polished walnut, with a tall back. Its overhanging canopy of shining wood almost touched the ceiling. Beneath that, three perfect little mirrors of thick glass were set into the rich walnut, and on either side of the music rack was a solid shelf for a lamp. The slanting music rack was of open woodwork cut in scrolls and backed with red cloth. It lifted on hinges, and revealed behind it a storage space for songbooks. Beneath this, the long, smooth lid folded back into the organ, or unfolded and dropped down to cover the row of black and white keys. Above the keys was a row of stops, marked tremolo and forte and other names, that changed the tone of the organ when they were pulled out. Underneath the keys were two levers that folded back against the organ, or opened so that a player's knees could work them. Pressed outward, they made the music louder. Just above the floor were two slanting pedals, covered with carpet, that a player's feet must press down and let up, to pump the organ.

With this beautiful organ, there was a walnut stool. It had a round top, standing on four curved legs. Grace was so excited about this stool that Laura could hardly look at the organ.

'Look, Laura, looky,' Grace said, and she sat on the

stool and whirled. The top of the stool worked on a screw, and it rose or sank under Grace as she whirled.

'We must not call this a claim shanty any more,' said Ma. 'It is a real house now, with four rooms.'

She had hung white muslin curtains at the windows; they were edged with white knitted lace. The black whatnot stood in the corner by the south window; the carved wooden bracket with the china shepherdess on it was hung on the eastern wall. The two rocking chairs sat comfortably by the east window and bright patchwork cushions lay on the wooden seat under the south window.

'What a pleasant place to sew in,' Ma said, looking at this new sitting room with a happy smile. 'I shall hurry your dress now, Laura. Perhaps I can have it finished by Sunday.'

'There is no hurry,' Laura told her. 'I don't want to wear it until I have my new hat. Miss Bell is making the very hat I want, but it will take two more Saturdays' work to pay for it.'

'Well, how do you like your organ, Laura?' Pa said, coming in from the stable. In the other room, which was only a kitchen now, Carrie was straining the milk.

'My goodness, Grace!' Ma exclaimed, just as Grace and the organ stool crashed on the floor. Grace sat up, too frightened to make a sound, and even Laura was horrified, for the stool lay in two pieces. Then Pa laughed.

'Never mind, Grace,' he said. 'You only unscrewed it all the way. But,' he said sternly, 'you stay off this stool, after this.'

'I will, Pa,' she said, trying to stand up. She was too dizzy. Laura set her on her feet and held her steady, and tried to say to Pa how much the organ pleased her. She could hardly wait until Mary came to play it while Pa played the fiddle.

At supper Ma said again that this was not a claim shanty any more. The kitchen was so spacious now, with only the stove, the cupboard, the table, and chairs in it.

'This won't be a claim, either, by year after next,' Pa reminded her. 'Another eighteen months, and I'll be able to prove up; it will be our land.'

'I hadn't forgotten, Charles,' said Ma. 'I'll be proud when we have our patent from the government. All the more reason to call this place a house, from now on.'

'And next year, if all goes well, I'm going to get it sided and painted,' Pa promised himself.

When Laura came home next Saturday she brought her new hat, after all. She carried it carefully, well wrapped in paper to protect it from dust.

'Miss Bell said I'd better take it, before someone else saw it and wanted it,' she explained. 'She says I can do the work for it afterwards, just as well.'

'You can wear it to church tomorrow,' Ma told her. 'For I have your dress finished.' The brown poplin was

161

laid out on Laura's bed, all pressed and shimmering, for her to see.

'Oh, let's see your hat, too,' Carrie asked, when they had all admired the dress, but Laura would not unwrap it.

'Not now,' she refused. 'I don't want you to see it, until I put it on with the dress.'

Next morning they were all up bright and early, to have time to get ready for church. It was a fresh, clear morning; the meadow larks were singing and the sunshine drinking the dew from the grass. All ready in her starched Sunday lawn and Sunday hair ribbons, Carrie sat carefully on her bed, to watch Laura dress.

'You do have beautiful hair, Laura,' she said.

'It isn't golden, like Mary's,' Laura answered. But in the sunshine as she brushed it, her hair was beautiful. It was fine, but very thick, and so long that the shimmering brown length of it, unbraided, fell below her knees. She brushed it back satin-smooth, and coiled and pinned the mass of braids. Then she took the curlers out of her bangs and carefully arranged the curly mass. She put on her knitted white-lace stockings, and buttoned her high, well-polished black shoes.

Then carefully over her under-petticoats she put on her hoops. She liked these new hoops. They were the very latest style in the East, and these were the first of the kind that Miss Bell had got. Instead of wires, there were wide tapes across the front, almost to her knees, holding the petticoats so that her dress would lie flat. These tapes held the wire bustle in place at the back, and it was an adjustable bustle. Short lengths of tape were fastened to either end of it; these could be buckled together underneath the bustle, to puff it out, either large or small. Or they could be buckled together in front, drawing the bustle down close behind, so that a dress rounded smoothly over it. Laura did not like a large bustle, so she buckled the tapes in front.

Then carefully over all she buttoned her best petticoat, and over all the starched petticoats she put on the underskirt of her new dress. It was of brown cambric, fitting smoothly around the top over the bustle, and gored to flare smoothly down over the hoops. At the bottom, just missing the floor, was a twelve-inch-wide flounce of the brown poplin, bound with an inch-wide band of plain brown silk. The poplin was not plain poplin, but striped with an openwork silk stripe.

Then over this underskirt and her starched white corset-cover, Laura put on the polonaise. Its smooth, long sleeves fitted her arms perfectly to the wrists, where a band of the plain silk ended them. The neck was high, with a smooth band of the plain silk around the throat. The polonaise fitted tightly and buttoned all down the front with small round buttons covered with the plain brown silk. Below the smooth hips it flared and rippled down and covered the top of the flounce on the underskirt. A band of the plain silk finished the polonaise at the bottom.

Around the brown silk neckband Laura placed a blue ribbon two inches wide. She pinned it together at her throat with the pearl bar pin that Ma had given her. The ends of the ribbon fell in streamers to her waist.

Then Laura unwrapped her hat. Carrie sighed with delight when she saw it.

It was a sage-green, rough straw, in poke-bonnet shape. It completely covered Laura's head and framed her face with its flaring brim. It was lined with shirred silk, blue. Wide blue ribbons tied under her left ear and held the bonnet securely in place.

The blue of the lining, the blue ribbon bow, and the blue neck ribbon, exactly matched the blue of Laura's eyes.

Pa and Ma and Grace were ready for church when she came out of the bedroom, with Carrie following her. Pa looked from the top of Laura's head to the bottom of the brown poplin flounce, where the soft black toes of her shoes peeped out. Then he said, 'They say that fine feathers make fine birds, but I say it took a fine bird to grow such feathers.'

Laura was so pleased that she could not speak.

'You look very nice,' Ma praised, 'but remember that pretty is as pretty does.'

'Yes, Ma,' Laura said.

'That's a funny hat,' said Grace.

'It isn't a hat. It's a poke bonnet,' Laura explained to her.

Then Carrie said, 'When I'm a young lady, I'm going to earn me a dress just exactly like that.'

'Likely you'll have a prettier one,' Laura answered quickly, but she was startled. She had not thought that she was a young lady. Of course she was, with her hair done up and her skirts almost touching the ground. She was not sure she liked being a young lady.

'Come,' Pa said. 'The team is waiting, and we'll be late to church if we don't hurry.'

The day was so pleasant and sunny that Laura hated to sit in the church, and Reverend Brown's long sermon seemed even duller than usual. The wild prairie grass was green outside the open windows and the light wind enticed her as it softly brushed her cheek. It seemed that there should be more, in such a day, than going to church and going home again.

Ma and Carrie and Grace changed at once into their everyday dresses, but Laura did not want to. She asked, 'May I keep my Sunday dress on, Ma? if I wear my big apron and am very careful?'

'You may if you want to,' Ma gave permission. 'No reason that anything should happen to your dress if you take care.'

After dinner, and after the dishes were washed, Laura wandered restlessly out of the house. The sky was so blue, the floating piles of cloud were so shimmering and pearly, and far and wide the land was green. In a row around the house the young cotton-woods were growing; the little saplings that Pa had planted were twice as tall as Laura now, spreading their slender branches and rustling leaves. They made a flickering shade in which Laura stood, looking east and south and west at the lovely, empty day.

She looked towards town, and while she looked a buggy came dashing around the corner by Pearson's livery barn and out along the road towards the Big Slough.

The buggy was new, for the sun flashed and sparkled from its wheels and top. The horses were brown and trotted evenly. Were they the colts that she had helped break? Surely, they were, and as they turned towards her and crossed the slough, she saw that Almanzo was driving them. They came trotting up, and the buggy stopped beside her.

'Would you like to go for a buggy ride?' Almanzo asked, and as Pa came out of the house Laura replied in the words she had always used.

'Oh yes! I'll be ready in a minute.'

She tied on her poke bonnet, and told Ma that she was going for a buggy ride. Carrie's eyes were shining, and she stopped Laura and stood tiptoe to whisper, 'Aren't you glad you didn't change your dress?'

'I am,' Laura whispered back, and she was. She was glad that her dress and her bonnet were so nice. Carefully Almanzo spread the linen lap robe, and she tucked it well under her flounce to cover the brown poplin from dust. Then they were driving away in the afternoon sunshine, southward towards the distant lakes, Henry and Thompson.

'How do you like the new buggy?' Almanzo asked.

It was a beautiful buggy, so black and shining, with glossy red spokes in the wheels. The seat was wide; at either end of it gleaming black supports slanted backward to the folded-down top behind, and the seat had a lazy-back, cushioned. Laura had never before been in a buggy so luxurious.

'It is nice,' Laura said, as she leaned comfortably back against the leather cushion. 'I never rode in a lazy-back buggy before. The back isn't quite as high as the plain wooden ones, is it?'

'Maybe this will make it better,' Almanzo said, laying his arm along the top of the back. He was not exactly hugging Laura, but his arm was against her shoulders. She shrugged, but his arm did not move away. So she leaned forward, and shook the buggy whip where it stood in the whipsocket on the dashboard. The colts jumped forward and broke into a run.

'You little devil!' Almanzo exclaimed, as he closed both hands on the lines and braced his feet. He needed both hands to control those colts.

After a time the colts were calmer and quieter, and trotting again.

'Suppose they had run away?' Almanzo then asked her indignantly.

'They could run a long way before they came to the end of the prairie,' Laura laughed. 'And there's nothing to run against between here and there.'

'Just the same!' Almanzo began, and then he said, 'You're independent, aren't you?'

'Yes,' said Laura.

They drove a long way that afternoon, all the way to Lake Henry and around it. Only a narrow tongue of land separated it from Lake Thompson. Between the sheets of blue water there was width enough only for a wagon track. Young cotton-woods and choke-cherry trees stood slim on either side, above a tangle of wild grapevines. It was cool there. The wind blew across the water, and between the trees they could see the little waves breaking against the shore on either side.

Almanzo drove slowly, as he told Laura of the eighty-acre field of wheat he had sown, and the thirty acres of oats.

'You know I have my homestead and my tree claim both to work on,' he said. 'Besides that, Cap and I have been hauling lumber for a long ways, out around town to build houses and schoolhouses all over the country. I had to team, to earn money for this new buggy.'

'Why not drive the one you had?' Laura sensibly wanted to know.

'I traded that on these colts last fall,' he explained. 'I

knew I could break them on the cutter in the winter, but when spring came, I needed a buggy. If I'd had one, I'd have been around to see you before this.'

As they talked, he drove out from between the lakes and around the end of Lake Henry, then away across the prairie to the north. Now and then they saw a little new claim shanty. Some had a stable, and a field of broken sod nearby.

'This country is settling up fast,' Almanzo said as they turned west along the shore of Silver Lake and so towards Pa's claim. 'We have driven only forty miles and we must have seen as many as six houses.'

The sun was low in the west when he helped her out of the buggy at her door.

'If you like buggy rides as well as sleigh rides, I will be back next Sunday,' he said.

'I like buggy rides,' Laura answered. Then suddenly she felt shy, and hurried into the house.

Nellie Oleson

'I declare,' Ma said. 'It never rains but it pours.' For strangely enough, Tuesday evening a young man who lived on a neighbouring claim came by, and asked Laura to go buggy riding with him next Sunday. On Thursday evening, another young neighbour asked her to go buggy riding with him next Sunday. And as she was walking home Saturday evening, a third young man overtook her and brought her home in his lumber wagon, and he asked her to go riding with him next day.

That Sunday Almanzo and Laura drove north past Almanzo's two claims, to Spirit Lake. There was a small claim shanty on Almanzo's homestead. On his tree claim there were no buildings at all; but the young trees were growing well. He had set them out carefully, and must cultivate and care for them for five years; then he could prove up on the claim and own the land. The trees were thriving much better than he had expected at first, for he said that if trees would grow on those prairies, he thought they would have grown there naturally before now.

'These government experts have got it all planned,' he

explained to Laura. 'They are going to cover these prairies with trees, all the way from Canada to Indian Territory. It's all mapped out in the land offices, where the trees ought to be, and you can't get that land except on tree claims. They're certainly right about one thing; if half these trees live, they'll seed the whole land and turn it into forest land, like the woods back East.'

'Do you think so?' Laura asked him in amazement. Somehow she could not imagine those prairies turned into woods, like Wisconsin.

'Well, time will show,' he answered. 'Anyway, I'm doing my part. I'll keep those trees alive if it can be done.'

Spirit Lake was beautiful and wild. There Almanzo drove along a rocky shore, where the water was deep and the waves ran foaming before the wind and dashed high on the rocks. There was an Indian mound by Spirit Lake, too. It was said to be a burial place, though no one knew what was in it. Tall cottonwoods grew there, and choke-cherries smothered in wild grapevines.

On the way back, they came into town past the Olesons' claim. It was on the section line a mile east of Almanzo's homestead. Laura had not seen Nellie Oleson's home before, and she felt a little sorry for her; the shanty was so small, standing among the wild grass in the wind. Mr Oleson had no horses, only a yoke of oxen, and the place was not improved as Pa's was. But Laura barely glanced at it, for she did not want to spoil the beautiful day by even thinking of Nellie Oleson.

'Good-bye, then, till next Sunday,' Almanzo said, as he left her at her door. The whole country seemed different to her, now that she had seen Lakes Henry and Thompson, and Spirit Lake with its strange Indian mound. She wondered what next Sunday would show.

Sunday afternoon as she watched the buggy coming across Big Slough she saw, to her surprise, that someone was with Almanzo. She wondered who it could be, and if perhaps he did not intend to go for a drive that day.

When the horses stopped at the door, she saw that Nellie Oleson was with him. Without waiting for him to speak, Nellie cried, 'Come on, Laura! Come with us for a buggy ride!'

'Want some help, Wilder?' Pa asked, going towards the colts' heads, and Almanzo said that he would be obliged. So Pa held the bridles, while Almanzo waited to help Laura into the buggy, and in stupefied surprise Laura let him. Nellie moved over to make room for her, and helped her tuck the lap robe around the brown poplin.

As they drove away, Nellie began to talk. She admired the buggy; she exclaimed over the colts; she praised Almanzo's driving; she gushed about Laura's clothes. 'Oh,' she said, 'Laura, your poke bonnet is just utterly too-too!' She never stopped for an answer. She did so want to see Lakes Henry and Thompson; she had heard so much about them; she thought the weather was just utterly too-too, and the country was nice, of course not anything like New York State, but that couldn't really be expected out West, could it?

'Why are you so quiet, Laura?' she asked without stopping and went on, with a giggle, 'My tongue wasn't made to lie still. My tongue's made to go flippity-flop!'

Laura's head ached; her ears rang with the continuous babble, and she was furious. Almanzo seemed to be enjoying the drive. At least, he looked as though he were being amused.

They drove to Lakes Henry and Thompson. They drove along the narrow tongue of land between them. Nellie thought the lakes were just utterly too-too; she liked lakes, she liked water, she liked trees and vines and she just adored driving on Sunday afternoons; she thought it was just too utterly too-too.

The sun was rather low as they came back, and since Laura's house was nearest, they stopped there first.

'I'll be along next Sunday,' Almanzo said as he helped Laura out of the buggy, and before Laura could speak, Nellie chimed in: 'Oh, yes! we will come by for you. Didn't you have a good time! Wasn't it fun! Till Sunday, then, don't forget, we'll be by, good-bye, Laura, good-bye!' Almanzo and Nellie drove away towards town.

All that week Laura debated with herself, to go or not to go. It was no pleasure to her to go driving with Nellie.

On the other hand, if she refused to go, Nellie would be pleased; that was what Nellie wanted. Trust Nellie to find some way to go driving with Almanzo every Sunday.

Laura made up her mind to go with them.

Next Sunday's drive began much like the one before. Nellie's tongue went flippity-flop. She was in gay spirits, chattering and laughing to Almanzo and almost ignoring Laura. She was sure of triumph, for she knew that Laura would not long endure this situation.

'Oh, Mannie, you have those wild colts so well broken, you handle them so wonderfully,' she cooed, leaning against Almanzo's arm.

Laura bent to tuck the dust robe more closely in at her feet, and as she straightened up again, she carelessly let the end of the robe flutter out on the strong prairie wind. The colts left the ground in one leap and ran.

Nellie screamed and screamed, clutching at Almanzo's arm, which he very much needed to use just then. Laura quietly tucked down the end of the lap robe and sat on it.

When it was no longer flapping behind them, the colts soon quieted and went on in their well-trained trot.

'Oh, I never was so frightened, I never was so frightened in my life,' Nellie chattered and gasped. 'Horses are such wild things. Oh, Mannie, why did they do it? Don't let them do it again.'

Almanzo looked sidewise at Laura and said nothing.

'Horses are all right if you understand them,' Laura

remarked. 'But I suppose these are not like the horses in New York.'

'Oh, I would never understand these western horses. New York horses are quiet,' Nellie said, and then she started talking of New York. She talked as though she knew it well. Laura knew nothing of New York State, but she knew that Nellie did not, either, and that Almanzo did.

They were nearing the turn towards home when Laura said, 'We are so near the Boasts'. Don't you think it would be nice to go see them?'

'If you like,' said Almanzo. Instead of turning west, he drove straight on north across the railroad tracks and farther out across the prairie to Mr Boast's homestead claim. Mr and Mrs Boast came out to the buggy.

'Well, well, so the buggy carries three,' Mr Boast teased, his black eyes sparkling. 'It's a wider seat than the cutter seat. The cutter was built for two.'

'Buggies are different,' Laura told him.

'They seem . . .' Mr Boast began, but Mrs Boast interrupted. 'Now, Rob!' she exclaimed. 'You'd better be asking the folks to get out and stay awhile.'

'We can't stay,' Laura said. 'We only stopped for a minute.'

'We are just out for a drive,' Almanzo explained.

'Then we will turn around here,' Nellie said with authority.

Laura spoke quickly, 'Let's go a little farther. I've never

been over this road. Is there time to go a little farther, Almanzo?'

'It's a good straight road north,' Mr Boast said. His eyes laughed at Laura. She was sure he guessed what was in her mind, and her eyes laughed back at him as Almanzo started the colts and they went on north. Beyond Mr Boast's claim they crossed an end of the Slough that ran northeast from Silver Lake. Here a road turned towards town, but it was wet and boggy as Laura had known it would be, so they kept on driving north.

'This is stupid, this isn't any fun; call this a good road?' Nellie fretted.

'It is good so far,' Laura said quietly.

'Well! we won't come this way again!' Nellie snapped. Then quickly she recovered her happy vivacity, telling Almanzo how much she enjoyed driving just anywhere with such a good driver and fine team.

Another road branched to the west and Almanzo turned the team into it. Nellie's home was only a little way ahead. As Almanzo helped her from the buggy at her door, she clung to his hand a moment, saying how much she had enjoyed the drive and, 'We'll go another way next Sunday, won't we, Mannie?'

'Oh, it's too bad I suggested going that way, Nellie, if you minded it so much,' said Laura, and Almanzo said only, 'Good-bye,' and took his place beside Laura.

There was quietness between them for a little while as

they drove towards town. Then Laura said, 'I am afraid I have made you late for your chores by wanting to take that road.'

'It doesn't matter,' he reassured her. 'The days and nights are as long as they ever were, and I don't have a cow.'

Again they were silent. Laura felt that she was dull company after Nellie's lively chatter, but she was determined that Almanzo would decide that. She would never try to hold him, but no other girl was going to edge her out little by little without his realizing it.

At home again, as Almanzo and Laura stood beside the buggy, he said, 'I suppose we'll go again next Sunday?'

'We'll not all go,' Laura answered. 'If you want to take Nellie for a drive, do so, but do not come by for me. Good night.'

She went quietly into the house and shut the door.

Sometimes when she was walking to her school, past the hollow that was growing greener with violets' leaves then blue with their blossoms, Laura wondered if Almanzo would come next Sunday. Sometimes when her three little pupils were diligently studying, she looked up from her own studies and saw the cloud shadows moving over the sunny grass beyond the windows, and wondered. If he didn't, he didn't; that was all. And she could only wait until next Sunday.

On Saturday she walked to town and sewed all day for

Miss Bell. Pa was breaking sod at home, to make a larger
wheat field, so Laura stopped at the post office to see if
there was any mail, and there was a letter from Mary! She
could hardly wait to get home to hear Ma read it, for it
would tell when Mary was coming home.

No one had written Mary about the new sitting room
and the organ that was waiting for her there. Never had
anyone in the family had such a surprise as that organ
would be for Mary.

'Oh, Ma! a letter from Mary!' she cried, bursting in.

'I'll finish the supper, Ma, you go read it,' said Carrie.
So Ma took a hairpin from her hair, and as she carefully slit
the envelope she sat down to read the letter. She unfolded
the sheet and began to read, and it was as if all the light
went out of the house.

Carrie gave Laura a frightened look, and after a moment Laura asked quietly, 'What is it, Ma?'

'Mary does not want to come home,' Ma said. Then, quickly, 'I do not mean that. She asks if she may spend her vacation with Blanche, at Blanche's home. Stir the potatoes, Carrie; they'll be too brown.'

All through supper they talked about it. Ma read the letter aloud. Mary wrote that Blanche's home was not far from Vinton, and she very much wanted that Mary should visit it. Her mother was writing to Ma, to invite Mary. Mary would like to go, if Pa and Ma said she might.

'I think she should,' Ma said. 'It will be a change for her, and do her good.'

Pa said, 'Well,' and so it was settled. Mary was not coming home that year.

Later, Ma said to Laura that Mary would be at home to stay when she finished college, and it might be that she would never have another opportunity to travel. It was nice that she could have this pleasant time and make so many new friends while she was young. 'She will have it to remember,' Ma said.

But that Saturday night, Laura felt that nothing would ever be right again. Next morning, though the sun was shining and the meadow larks singing, they did not mean anything, and as she rode to church in the wagon she said to herself that she would ride in a wagon all the rest of her life. She was quite sure now that Almanzo would take Nellie Oleson driving that day.

Still, at home again she did not take off her brown poplin, but put her big apron on as she had done before. Time went very slowly, but at last it was two o'clock, and looking from the window Laura saw the colts come dashing over the road from town. They trotted up and stopped at the door.

'Would you like to go for a buggy ride?' Almanzo asked, as Laura stood in the doorway.

'Oh, yes!' Laura answered. 'I'll be ready in a minute.' Her face looked at her from the mirror, all rosy and smiling, as she tied the blue ribbon bow under her left ear.

In the buggy she asked, 'Wouldn't Nellie go?'

'I don't know,' Almanzo replied. After a pause he said in disgust: 'She is afraid of horses.' Laura said nothing, and in a moment he continued, 'I wouldn't have brought her the first time, but I overtook her walking in the road. She was walking all the way to town to see someone, but she said she'd rather go along with us. Sundays at her house are so long and lonely that I felt sorry for her, and she seemed to enjoy the drive so much. I didn't know you girls disliked each other.'

Laura was amazed that a man who knew so much about farming and horses could know so little about a girl like Nellie. But she said only, 'No, you wouldn't know, because you did not go to school with us. I will tell you what I'd like to do, I'd like to take Ida driving.'

'We will, sometime,' Almanzo agreed. 'But today is pretty fine, just by ourselves.'

It was a beautiful afternoon. The sun was almost too warm, and Almanzo said that the colts were so well broken now that they could raise the buggy top. So together, each with a hand, they raised it and pressed the hinge of the braces straight to hold it up. Then they rode in its shade with the gentle wind blowing through the open sides.

After that day, nothing was ever said about the next Sunday, but always at two o'clock Almanzo drove around the corner of Pearson's livery barn, and Laura was ready when he stopped at the door. Pa would look up from his paper and nod good-bye to her, then go on reading, and Ma would say, 'Don't be out too late, Laura.'

June came and the wild prairie roses bloomed. Laura and Almanzo gathered them beside the road and filled the buggy with the fragrant blossoms.

Then one Sunday at two o'clock the corner of Pearson's barn remained empty. Laura could not imagine what might have happened, till suddenly the colts were at the door, and Ida was in the buggy, laughing merrily.

Almanzo had gone by the Reverend Brown's, and persuaded Ida to come. Then, for a surprise, he had crossed the Big Slough west of the town road; this brought them to Pa's land a little south of the house, and while Laura watched towards the north, they had come up from the opposite direction.

They drove that day to Lake Henry, and it was the merriest of drives. The colts behaved beautifully. They stood quietly while Ida and Laura filled their arms with the wild roses and climbed back into the buggy. They nibbled at the bushes by the road while Almanzo and the girls watched the little waves ripple along the shores of the lakes on either hand.

The road was so narrow and so low that Laura said, 'I should think the water might be over the road sometimes.'

'Not since I have known it,' Almanzo answered, 'but perhaps, many years or ages ago, the two lakes were one.'

Then for a while they sat in silence and Laura thought how wild and beautiful it must have been when the twin lakes were one, when buffalo and antelope roamed the prairie around the great lake and came there to drink, when wolves and coyotes and foxes lived on the banks and wild geese, swans, herons, cranes, ducks, and gulls nested and fished and flew there in countless numbers.

'Why did you sigh?' Almanzo asked.

'Did I?' said Laura. 'I was thinking that wild things leave when people come. I wish they wouldn't.'

'Most people kill them,' he said.

'I know,' Laura said. 'I can't understand why.'

'It is beautiful here,' said Ida, 'but we are a long way from home and I promised Elmer I'd go to church with him tonight.'

Almanzo tightened the reins and spoke to the colts while Laura asked, 'Who's Elmer?'

'He is a young man who has a claim near Father Brown's and he boards at our place,' Ida told her. 'He wanted me to go walking with him this afternoon, but I thought I'd rather go with you, this once. You've never seen Elmer . . . McConnell,' she remembered to add.

'There are so many new people, and I can't keep track of the ones I know,' Laura said.

'Mary Power is going with the new clerk in Ruth's bank,' Ida told her.

'But Cap!' Laura exclaimed. 'What about Cap Garland?'

'Cap's smitten with a new girl who lives west of town,' Almanzo told them.

'Oh, I think it's a pity we don't all go in a crowd any more,' Laura lamented. 'What fun the sleighing parties were, and now everyone's paired off.'

'Oh, well,' Ida said. '"In the spring a young man's fancy lightly turns to thoughts of love."'

'Yes, or it's this,' and Laura sang,

'Oh whistle and I'll come to you, my lad,
Oh whistle and I'll come to you, my lad,
Though father and mither and a' should
    gae mad,
Oh whistle and I'll come to you, my lad.'

'Would you?' Almanzo asked.

'Of course not!' Laura answered. 'That's only a song.'

'Better whistle for Nellie, she'd come,' Ida teased, and then she said soberly, 'But she is afraid of these horses. She says they aren't safe.'

Laura laughed delightedly. 'They were a little wild, the time she was with us,' she said.

'But I can't understand it. They are perfectly gentle,' Ida insisted.

Laura only smiled and tucked the dust robe in more securely. Then she saw Almanzo looking sidewise at her behind Ida's head, and she let her eyes twinkle at him. She didn't care if he did know that she had frightened the colts to scare Nellie, on purpose.

All the miles home they rode talking and singing, until they came to Laura's home, and as she left them she asked, 'Won't you come with us next Sunday, Ida?'

Blushing, Ida answered, 'I would like to, but I . . . I think I'm going walking with Elmer.'

21

Barnum and Skip

June was gone, and Laura's school was out. The organ was paid for. Laura learned to play a few chords with Pa's fiddle, but she would rather listen to the fiddle alone, and after all, the organ was for Mary's enjoyment when Mary came home.

One evening Pa said, 'Tomorrow's Fourth of July. Do you girls want to go to the celebration in town?'

'Oh no, let's have it as it was last year,' Carrie said. 'I don't want to be in a crowd where they shoot off firecrackers. I'd rather have our own firecrackers at home.'

'I want lots of candy at home,' Grace put in her vote.

'I suppose Wilder will be around with that team and buggy, Laura?' Pa asked.

'He didn't say anything about it,' Laura answered. 'But I don't want to go to the celebration, anyway.'

'Is this unanimous, Caroline?' Pa wanted to know.

'Why, yes, if you agree with the girls,' Ma smiled at them all. 'I will plan a celebration dinner, and the girls will help me cook it.'

All the next morning they were very busy. They baked

fresh bread, a rhubarb pie, and a two-egg cake. Laura went to the garden, and with her fingers dug carefully into the hills of potatoes to find new potatoes. She gathered enough potatoes for dinner, without injuring one plant by disturbing its roots. Then she picked the first of the green peas, carefully choosing only the plump pods.

Ma finished frying a spring chicken while the new potatoes and the peas were cooked and given a cream dressing. The Fourth of July dinner was just ready, all but steeping the tea, when Pa came home from town. He brought lemons for afternoon lemonade, firecrackers for the evening, and candy for all the time after dinner.

As he gave the packages to Ma, he said to Laura, 'I saw Almanzo Wilder in town. He and Cap Garland were hitching up a new team he's got. That young fellow missed his vocation; he ought to be a lion tamer. Those horses are wilder than hawks. It was all he and Cap could do to handle them. He said to tell you if you want to go for a buggy ride this afternoon, be ready to climb in when he drives up, for he won't be able to get out to help you. Said to tell you, there's another team to break.'

'I do believe he wants to break your neck!' said Ma. 'And I hope he breaks his own, first.'

This was so unlike Ma's gentle self that they all stared at her.

'Wilder will manage the horses, Caroline. Don't worry,' Pa said confidently. 'If ever I saw a born horseman, he's one.'

'Do you really not want me to go, Ma?' Laura asked.

'You must use your own judgement, Laura,' Ma replied. 'Your Pa says it is safe, so it must be.'

After they had slowly enjoyed that delicious dinner, Ma told Laura to leave the dishes and go put on her poplin if she intended to go driving. 'I'll do up the work,' Ma said.

'But you have worked all morning,' Laura objected. 'I can do it and still have time to dress.'

'Neither of you need bother about the dishes,' Carrie spoke up. 'I'll wash, and Grace will wipe. Come on, Grace. You and I are older than Mary and Laura were when they did the work.'

So Laura was ready and waiting at the door when Almanzo came. She had never seen the horses before. One was a tall bay, with black mane and tail. The other was a large brown horse, spotted with white. On one side of his brown neck a white spot resembled a rooster. A streak of white in the brown mane looked like the rooster's tail.

Almanzo stopped this strange team and Laura went towards the buggy, but the brown horse reared straight up on his hind legs, with front feet pawing the air, while the bay horse jumped ahead. Almanzo loosened the reins and as the horses sprang away he called, 'I'll be back.'

Laura waited while he drove around the house. When he stopped the horses again, she went quickly to the buggy, but stepped back as again the spotted horse reared and the bay jumped.

Pa and Ma were beside Laura; Carrie stood in the doorway clutching a dish towel, and Grace looked out beside her. They all waited while Almanzo drove around the house again.

Ma said, 'You'd better not try to go, Laura,' but Pa told her, 'Caroline, she will be all right. Wilder will handle them.'

This time as Almanzo stopped the horses he turned them a little, cramping the buggy to give Laura a better chance to get between the wheels. 'Quick,' he said.

Hoops and all, Laura moved quickly. Her right hand grasped the folded-down braces of the buggy top, her right foot touched the buggy step, and as the spotted horse reared and the bay horse leaped, her left foot stepped into the buggy and she dropped into the seat. 'Drat these hoops!' she muttered, while she settled them inside the speeding buggy, and covered her brown poplin with the dust robe.

'Don't touch the buggy top!' Almanzo said, and then they were silent. He was fully occupied in keeping control of the horses, and Laura made herself small on her side of the seat to keep out of the way of his straining arms as he tried to pull the horses down out of their run.

They went north because they were headed that way. As they streaked through town Laura caught a glimpse of a thickly scrambling crowd getting out of the way, and Cap Garland's grin as he waved his hand to her.

189

Later she thought with satisfaction that she had sewed the ribbon ties to her poke bonnet herself; she was sure the stitches would not give way.

The horses settled to a fast trot, and Almanzo remarked, 'They said you wouldn't go, and Cap said you would.'

'Did he bet I would?' Laura asked.

'I didn't, if that's what you want to know,' Almanzo answered. 'I wouldn't bet about a lady. Anyway, I wasn't sure how you'd like this circus I'm driving.'

'What became of the colts?' Laura inquired.

'I sold them.'

'But Prince and Lady . . .' Laura hesitated. 'I am not criticizing these horses, I just wondered if anything is wrong with Prince and Lady.'

'Nothing is wrong. Lady has a colt and Prince doesn't drive so well without Lady. I had an offer of three hundred dollars for the colts, they're a well-matched, well-broken team and worth it, but you can't be sure of a fair price every day. This team cost me only two hundred. That's a clear gain of a hundred dollars, and I figure I can sell these for more than they cost me, if I want to, when they're broken. I think it will be fun to break them, don't you?'

'Oh, yes!' Laura answered. 'We will teach them to be gentle.'

'That's what I figured. By the way, the spotted one's named Barnum, and the bay is Skip. We won't go by the picnic grounds; the firecrackers would make them wild again,' Almanzo said.

The horses went on mile after mile at a swift trot on the road across the open prairie. Rain had fallen the night before and water stood in pools wherever the road dipped, but Barnum and Skip refused to get their feet wet. They jumped across every puddle, taking the buggy flying over it with them and not a spatter fell on Laura's poke bonnet.

The Fourth of July sun was hot, and Laura wondered why Almanzo did not suggest raising the buggy top until he said, 'I'm sorry, but if we raised the top these horses would be frantic. I don't know if I could hold them. Cap and I together couldn't hitch them to the buggy till we put the top down.'

So they rode in the sunshine with the prairie wind blowing and white clouds sailing the blue sky overhead. They drove to Spirit Lake, around the end of it and beyond; then by different roads they went home again.

'We have driven sixty miles,' Almanzo said as they neared the house. 'I think the horses will stand to let you out. I daren't get out to help you, for fear they would leave me.'

'I can get out myself,' Laura said. 'Don't let the horses get away. But won't you stay to supper?'

'I'd like to, but I must get the horses back to town before I stop them, so Cap can help me unhitch. Here we are. Don't jiggle the buggy top as you step down between the wheels.'

Laura tried not to, but she did jar it a little; Barnum reared, Skip leaped, and they dashed away.

When Almanzo came next Sunday, Laura knew what to expect. She was quick to spring into the buggy the first time the horses stopped.

They were headed east, and they ran that way. After a while they went more quietly, and Almanzo drove them by a roundabout way to the twin lakes. Rapidly, but without rearing or plunging, they passed over the narrow road between the lakes, and on the homeward road they trotted.

'I have been driving them some this week, and I guess they are beginning to get the idea that they might as well behave,' Almanzo remarked.

'But they are not as much fun when they behave,' Laura complained.

'You think not? Well, then let's teach them what a buggy top is for. Catch hold!'

Barely in time to do her part, Laura caught the front brace at her side of the buggy top and lifted it as Almanzo lifted his side. Quickly she pressed back on the hinge in its middle, straightening and clamping it as Almanzo did. The top was up and held firmly in place, just in the nick of time.

Skip sprang, and Laura caught her breath as Barnum reared. Up and up he went, forefeet pawing the air higher still, and his huge back rising in front of the dashboard.

Nearer it came and nearer, in one more instant it would topple backward upon the buggy. Then with a great leap Barnum came down, far ahead, running with Skip. The buggy top swayed with the swiftness of its going and fear of it increased their speed.

Almanzo's arms were rigid as he held the reins that were taut and straight as wires. Laura shrank back in her corner of the seat, held her breath, and hoped they would not break.

At last the horses tired, and slowed to a trot. Almanzo drew a deep breath and relaxed a little. 'Was that better?' he smiled at Laura.

Laura laughed shakily. 'Much better, so long as the harness holds together,' she said.

'The harness will hold. I had it made to order at Schaub's harness shop. Every strap is sound leather and it's double-riveted and wax-sewed. In time these horses will learn the difference between running and running away,' he said confidently. 'They were runaways, you know.'

'Were they?' said Laura, and her laugh was still a little shaky.

'Yes, that's why I got them so cheap. They can run, but they can't run away from us. After a while they'll learn that they can't, and they'll stop trying and be a good team.'

'The buggy top is still up, and still scaring them. How will we ever get it down?' Laura wanted to know.

'We don't need to put it down. Just be careful not to

shake it when you're getting out, and I'll leave it up.'

The dangerous instant, in getting in or out of the buggy, was the instant that she was between the wheels. She had to be quicker than the horses, and go between the wheels without being caught.

When Almanzo stopped the horses at her door, very carefully Laura stooped under the buggy top's braces without touching them, and quickly she got to the ground. Her skirts swooshed as she went, and the horses jumped and were gone.

She was surprised that her knees felt weak as she went into the house. Pa turned to look at her.

'Safely home again,' he said.

'There isn't a bit of danger,' Laura told him.

'No, of course not, but just the same I shall feel better when those horses are quieter. I suppose you're going again next Sunday?'

'I think so,' Laura answered.

Next Sunday the horses were much quieter. They stood while Laura got into the buggy. Then quickly they started and trotted swiftly away. Almanzo drove them through town and northward. As the miles slipped behind them, their shining coats became dark with sweat.

Almanzo gently tried to pull them back to a walk. 'Better slow down, boys, you'll be cooler if you do,' he told them, but they refused to slacken their speed. 'Oh, well, if you want to go, it won't hurt you,' he added.

'It is terribly warm,' Laura said, raising the bangs from her forehead to let the wind blow underneath them. The heat of the sun was intense and strangely smothering.

'We can raise the top,' Almanzo said, but doubtfully.

'Oh, no, let's don't!' Laura objected. 'The poor things are warm enough, without running away . . . without running,' she corrected herself.

'It is pretty warm to excite them so much,' Almanzo agreed. 'It might not hurt them, but I'd rather not risk it, if you don't mind the sun.'

As time passed the horses trotted more slowly. Still they would not walk, but trotted onward steadily until Laura suggested turning homeward earlier than usual because of the weather signs.

The wind came in short, hot puffs from every direction, and thunderclouds were in the west. Almanzo agreed, 'It does look like rain.'

Turned towards home, the horses trotted more swiftly, but it was a long way to go. Ghostly whirlwinds sped invisible over the prairie, twisting the grass in small circles as they went, as if unseen fingers were stirring it.

'Dust devils,' Almanzo remarked, 'only there is no dust, nothing but grass. They say they're a sure sign of cyclone weather.'

The thunderheads piled up in the west; the whole sky looked stormy. The sun was shooting angry red beams of light across the dark clouds when Laura came home.

Almanzo hurried away to reach his claim and make things snug there before the rain fell.

But the storm held off. Night came, black and oppressive, with still no rain, and Laura slept uneasily. Suddenly she woke in a glare of light; Ma stood by the bedside, holding a lamp. She shook Laura's shoulder.

'Quick, Laura!' she said. 'Get up and help Carrie get her clothes, and come! Pa says there's a bad storm coming.'

Laura and Carrie snatched up their clothes and followed Ma, who had snatched up Grace and her clothes and a blanket and was hurrying to the open trapdoor of the cellar.

'Go down, girls, quickly. Hurry,' she told them. They tumbled hastily down into the small cellar under the kitchen.

'Where is Pa?' Laura asked.

Ma blew out the lamp. 'He is outdoors, watching the cloud. He can get here quickly, now that we are all down out of his way.'

'Why did you blow out the lamp, Ma?' Grace almost whimpered.

'Get into your clothes as well as you can, girls.' Ma said. 'We don't want the lamp, Grace; we don't want any risk of fire.'

They could hear the roaring of wind, and a strange wild note was in it. Flashes of lightning glared into the darkness. The kitchen overhead was brighter than fire for an instant, then the dark was blacker and seemed to press on the eyeballs.

Ma dressed Grace, while Laura and Carrie somehow got into their clothes. Then they all sat on the earth floor, with their backs against the earth wall, and waited.

Laura knew they were safer in the cellar, but she could hardly bear the closed-in, underground feeling of it. She wanted to be out in the wind with Pa, watching the storm. The wind roared. The lightning slapped her open eyes with glare and darkness. Overhead in the kitchen the clock, pathetically ignorant of the storm, struck one.

It seemed a long time before Pa's voice came down through the darkness. 'You may come up now, Caroline. The storm passed west of us, between here and the Wessington Hills.'

'Oh, Pa, it wasn't near enough to get the Reverend Brown's, was it?' Laura asked.

'No. I doubt if this house would have stood if it had come that near,' Pa answered.

Cramped and chilled from sitting so long uncomfortably in the cold cellar, they all crawled wearily into their beds.

All through August the weather was hot, and there were many thunderstorms. Several times Ma roused Laura and Carrie in the night, to go down cellar with her and Grace while Pa watched the storm clouds. The wind blew with terrific force, but it was always a straight wind; and the worst of it passed to the west.

Frightened as she was in these terrifying nights, Laura felt a strange delight in the wild strength of the wind, the terrible beauty of the lightning, and the crashes of thunder.

But in the morning they were all tired and heavy-eyed. Pa said, 'It seems we have to have about so many electric storms. If we don't get them in blizzards in the wintertime, we get them in cyclones and thunderstorms in the summer.'

'We can't do anything about it, so we must take them as they come,' said Ma.

Pa rose from the table, and stretched as he yawned. 'Well, I can make up my sleep when the cyclone season is over. Right now I have to cut the oats,' and he went out to his work.

He was cutting the oats and wheat again with the old cradle. A harvester cost more money than he had, and he would not go in debt for one.

'This giving a mortgage on everything he owns, to buy a two-hundred-dollar machine, and paying ten per cent interest on the debt, will ruin a man,' he said. 'Let these brash young fellows go in debt for machinery and break up all their land. I'm going to let the grass keep on growing, and raise cattle.'

Since he had sold Ellen's big calf to send Mary to college, he had bought another cow. Ellen's little calf had grown up, other calves had grown up, until now he had six cows and heifers, besides this year's calves, so he needed a great deal of grass and hay.

On the last Sunday in August, Almanzo came driving Barnum single. Barnum reared, but Laura was quick, and when his feet touched the ground again she was safely in the buggy seat.

When Barnum had almost reached town and had settled to a trot, Almanzo explained. 'I want to break him to drive single. He is so large and strong and such a good-looker that he will be worth more as a single driver than in a team. He must get over this way of starting, though.'

'He is a beauty,' Laura agreed, 'and I believe he is really gentle. Let me drive him; I would like to see if I could.'

Almanzo seemed doubtful, but he gave her the lines. 'Keep a tight rein on him,' he said. 'Don't let him get the start of you.'

Laura had not realized before how very small her hands were. They looked and felt tiny, holding those leather lines, but she was strong. She drove around the corner by the livery barn and all the way up Main Street, Barnum trotting as fast as he could.

'Did you see them turn and stare?' said Almanzo. 'They never expected to see a woman driving that horse.'

Laura saw nothing but Barnum. Across the railroad tracks and on through Poverty Flat, the new part of town, she drove. But her arms were growing tired, and a little way out of town she gave the lines back to Almanzo.

'When my arms are rested, I want to drive again,' she told him.

'You may,' he promised. 'You may drive all you want to. It gives my arms a rest, too.'

The next time she took the lines they felt alive. Through them she got the feel of Barnum's mouth. A kind of thrill came up the lines to her hands. 'I do believe Barnum knows I'm driving,' she said in surprise.

'Of course he does. He doesn't pull so hard, either. Watch him!' Almanzo took the lines. At once they grew tauter and seemed almost to stretch.

'He leans on the bit, with me,' Almanzo said. Abruptly he changed the subject. 'Do you know your old schoolteacher, Clewett, is going to start a singing school?'

Laura had not heard this. Almanzo said, 'I'd like to have you go with me, if you will.'

'I would like to, very much,' she answered.

'All right, next Friday night. I'll come for you at seven.' Almanzo went on, 'He's got to learn to walk. He's never been known to walk yet when he was hitched up. Seems to think that if he can keep on going fast enough he can get away from the buggy.'

'Let me take him again,' Laura said. She loved the feel of Barnum's mouth coming to her hands through the lines. It was true that he did not pull so hard when she was driving him. 'He is really gentle,' she said again, though she knew that he had always been a runaway.

All that afternoon she took turns with Almanzo, driving, and before he stopped to let her out at home, he reminded her, 'Friday night, at seven. I'll be driving Barnum single, and he may act up, so be ready.'

22

Singing School

School began next day in the new brick schoolhouse on Third Street in town. This was a two-storey schoolhouse, with two teachers. The small children were in the downstairs room, and the older ones upstairs.

Laura and Carrie were in the upstairs room. It seemed strangely large and empty, without the small children. Yet almost all the seats were filled with boys and girls whom they did not know. Only a few back seats were empty, and these would be filled when the weather grew too cold for farm work and the big boys came to school.

At recess Ida and Laura stood at an upstairs window, looking down at the children playing outdoors and talking with Mary Power and Minnie Johnson. Ida and Elmer were coming to the singing school Friday night, and so were Minnie and her brother, Arthur, and Mary Power with her new beau, Ed.

'I wonder why Nellie Oleson isn't coming to school,' Laura wondered, and Ida said, 'Oh, hadn't you heard? She's gone back to New York.'

'Not really!'

'Yes, she's gone back there to stay with some relatives. You know what I bet, I bet she talks all the time about how wonderful it is in the West!' Ida laughed. They all laughed.

All alone among the empty seats one of the new girls was sitting by herself. She was very blonde, and tall and slender, and she looked unhappy. Suddenly Laura knew how she felt.

They were all having such a good time, and there she sat, left out and lonely and shy, as Laura used to feel.

'That new girl looks nice, and she looks lonesome,' Laura said in a low voice. 'I'm going to go talk to her.'

The new girl's name was Florence Wilkins. Her father had a claim northwest of town, and she intended to be a schoolteacher. Laura had been sitting with her and talking only a little while, when the others came from the window and gathered around them. Florence was not coming to the singing school. She lived too far away.

On Friday evening, Laura was ready promptly at seven, in her brown poplin and her brown velvet hat, and promptly at seven Almanzo came. Barnum stopped, and Laura jumped into the buggy so quickly that Almanzo started him again before he had time to rear.

'That's the first time,' Almanzo said. 'He's getting slower about rearing. Maybe sometime he'll forget it.'

'Maybe,' Laura doubted it. She quoted, '"May bees don't fly in September."'

Singing school was to be in the church, and as they came into town Almanzo said that they would better leave a little early, before the others came out, because a crowd around Barnum would excite him. Laura replied, 'When you think it is time, just leave, and I will come.'

Almanzo tied Barnum to one of the hitching posts, and they went into the lighted church. He had paid tuition for two, and bought a singing book. The class was already there, and Mr Clewett was seating them. He placed the bass singers in a group, the tenors in another, and sopranos and altos in groups.

Then he taught them the names and values of the notes, the holds, the slurs, and the rests, and the bass, tenor, and treble clefs. After this, he allowed a short recess, and basses, altos, tenors, and sopranos all mixed together, talking and laughing, until Mr Clewett called them to order again.

They practised singing scales. Mr Clewett gave the

pitch with his tuning fork again and again. When almost all of them managed to sound very nearly the same note, they were off, up and down the scale, singing 'do, re, mi, fa, sol, la, si, do'. Exhausted from climbing so high, the voices all gladly came down again, 'Do, si, la, sol, fa, mi, re, do!'

Up and down and up and down they sang, sometimes striking the notes and sometimes not, but always with a good will. Laura had taken a place at the end of a seat, and she watched for a sign from Almanzo. When quietly he went to the door, she slipped away and followed.

While they hurried to the buggy he said, 'I'll help you in before I untie him. Likely he'll rear as soon as he is untied, but not before if you don't tighten the lines. Take a good hold on them, but don't move them until he starts. I'll try to get in before he comes down, but if I can't make it, you must hold him. Let him run, but don't let him run away. Drive him around the church and pass me again. Don't be afraid, you can drive him. You have, you know.'

She had never driven him when he was starting, Laura thought, though she said nothing. Climbing quickly into the buggy, she took hold of the lines where they lay across the dashboard. She gripped them tightly but did not move them.

At the hitching post, Almanzo untied Barnum. The instant his head was free, Barnum reared. Up and up he went until he stood straight on his hind legs; he was down

again and running before Laura could catch her breath. The buggy wheels left the ground and struck it with a jolt.

Laura held firmly to the lines. Barnum was racing away on the open prairie beyond the church. She pulled steadily harder with her right arm than with the left, and to her joy Barnum turned that way. He came swiftly around in a very neat circle. The church whirled in its centre, and as its side turned towards her, Laura pulled with all her strength on both lines evenly. But Barnum did not stop. They flashed past Almanzo, still standing at the hitching post.

With Barnum's first leap, Laura's heart had leaped too, up into her throat where it nearly choked her. Now they were out on the prairie again. She pulled steadily on the right-hand line, and again Barnum turned. Very quickly the other side of the church was coming towards her, and

Laura pulled on both lines. Barnum almost paused, then with a rearing plunge he was running again.

This time Laura's heart stayed in its place. She pulled with her right arm, and Barnum circled neatly. They passed around the church, and Laura rose a little from the seat. With all her weight she pulled. And Barnum stopped. He reared at once, and leaped and ran.

'All right, run,' Laura thought. She held him firmly; she guided him around the circle on the prairie, and again she braced her feet and pulled with all her might. This time, Almanzo got into the buggy. As he did so, the church door opened. All the singing-school pupils came pouring out, and someone shouted, 'Need help?'

Barnum rose straight up in the air, and came down running.

Almanzo's hands closed on the lines ahead of Laura's, and slid back as she let go. She was glad to let him have the lines.

'Just in time,' he said. 'We never would have got away if that crowd had swarmed around us. Was it too much for you?'

Laura was shaking. Her hands were numb, and it was hard to keep her teeth from chattering, so she only said, 'Oh, no.'

For a moment or two Almanzo spoke to Barnum, who soon began to trot. Then Laura said, 'Barnum wasn't bad. He was just tired of standing still so long.'

'He was plain mad about it,' Almanzo said. 'Next time we'll leave at recess.' He added, 'Let's go home the long way, it is such a nice night for a drive.'

He turned Barnum to the road that crossed the western end of Big Slough. The wind blew softly in the prairie grass, and above the dark land hung myriads of large stars quivering with light.

On and on Barnum trotted, gently now as if he, too, were enjoying the quietness of the night and the brilliant stars.

Almanzo spoke quietly. 'I don't know when I ever saw the stars so bright.'

Then Laura began to sing softly:

'In the starlight, in the starlight,
Let us wander gay and free,
For there's nothing in the daylight
Half so dear to you and me.
Like the fairies in the shadow
Of the woods we'll steal along,
And our sweetest lays we'll warble,
For the night was made for song.
When none are by to listen,
Or to chide us in our glee,
In the starlight, in the starlight,
Let us wander, gay and free.'

Barnum stopped at the door and stood quietly while Laura got out. Almanzo said, 'I'll be along Sunday afternoon.'

'I will be ready,' Laura answered. Then she went in.

Pa and Ma were waiting up for her. Ma gave a little sigh of relief, and Pa asked, 'Does that devil horse of Wilder's drive all right at night?'

'He is really a gentle horse,' said Laura. 'And he stood so quietly when I got out. I like him.'

Ma was satisfied, but Pa looked at her sharply. It was not a lie; she had spoken the truth, and she could not tell them how she had driven Barnum. That would worry them, and perhaps they would forbid her to do it again. She intended to drive Barnum. When she and Barnum were used to each other, perhaps, just perhaps, she could make him act gently.

23

Barnum Walks

Next Sunday Barnum was as bad as he had ever been. He refused to stand, and Laura had to wait for a third stop before she could leap into the buggy. Then he reared and tried to run, pulling so hard that after a time Almanzo complained, 'He is pulling this buggy by the bit and my arms.'

'Let me try,' Laura offered. 'It will rest your arms.'

'All right,' Almanzo agreed. 'For a minute, but you'll have to hold hard.'

He let go of the lines when she had a firm grip on them, just behind his. Laura's arms took the force of Barnum's pull; his strength flowed up the lines with the thrill she had felt before. Oh, Barnum! she begged silently; please don't pull so hard, I want so much to drive you.

Barnum sensed the change of drivers and stretched his neck a little farther, feeling the bit; then his trot became slower. He turned the corner by the livery barn, and dropped into a walk.

Barnum was walking. Almanzo was silent and Laura hardly breathed. A little by a tiny little she eased on the lines. Barnum went on walking. The wild horse, the runaway, who never before had been seen to walk when hitched to a buggy, walked the whole length of Main Street. He reached out twice, feeling the bit with his mouth and, finding it to his liking, arched his neck and walked proudly on.

Almanzo said, low, 'Better tighten the lines a little so he won't get the jump on you.'

'No,' Laura answered. 'I am going to let him carry the bit easily. I think he likes it.'

All along the street, everyone stopped to stare. Laura did not like to be so conspicuous, but she knew that she must not be nervous now; she must be calm, and keep Barnum walking. 'I wish they wouldn't stare,' she almost whispered, looking straight ahead at Barnum's placid ears.

In a low tone, too, Almanzo replied, 'They have been expecting he would run away with us. Better not let him walk until he starts trotting himself. Tighten the lines and tell him to go. Then he will understand that he trots because you want him to.'

'You take him,' Laura offered. She felt a little dizzy from the excitement.

Almanzo took the lines and at his command Barnum trotted.

'Well, I'll be darned! how did you do it?' he asked then. 'I've been trying ever since I've had him to get him to walk. What did you do?'

'I didn't do anything,' Laura said. 'He is really a gentle horse.'

All the rest of that afternoon, Barnum walked or trotted when told to do so, and Almanzo bragged, 'He'll be gentle as a lamb after this.'

He was mistaken. On Friday night Barnum again refused to stand, and when finally Laura landed in the buggy, Almanzo reminded her that they would leave singing school at recess. But, though Barnum had not been tied so long as before, he was in such a temper that Laura drove him around and around the church until they barely got away as singing school was over.

Laura loved singing school. It began with singing scales to limber up the voices. Then Mr Clewett taught them a simple exercise, the first in the book. He gave them the pitch with his tuning fork again and again, until all their voices chimed with it. Then they sang:

> 'Gaily now our boat is sailing,
> O'er the blue and sparkling wave.'

When they could sing this very well, they learned another. This was the song of the grass:

'All around the open door
– Smiling on the rich and poor,
Here I come! Here I come!
Creeping everywhere.'

Then they sang rounds:

'Three blind mice, see how they run,
they all ran after the farmer's wife
she cut off their tails with a carving
knife three blind mice see how they
run they all ran after . . .'

The basses chased the tenors that chased the altos that chased the sopranos around and around until they were all lost and exhausted from laughing. It was such fun! Laura could last longer than anyone because Pa had taught her and Carrie and Grace to sing 'Three Blind Mice' long ago.

Barnum grew so gentle that Laura and Almanzo could stay till the evening's end, and at recess he and the other young men took striped paper bags of candy from their coat pockets and passed them around to the girls. There were pink-and-white striped peppermint balls, and sticks of lemon candy and peppermint candy and horehound candy. And on the way home Laura sang:

'Oh childhood's joys are very great,
A-swingin' on his mother's gate,
A-eatin' candy till his mouth
Is all stuck up from north to south,
But though I have to mind the rule,
I'd rather go to singing school!'

'That's why I thought you'd like to go,' Almanzo said. 'You're always singing.'

Each singing-school night the class sang farther and farther over in the book. On the last night they sang the anthem at the very end; page one hundred forty-four, 'The Heavens Declare the Glory'.

Then singing school was ended. There would be no more such gay evenings.

Barnum no longer reared and plunged. He started quickly, with a little jump, into a smooth trot. The air was chilled with the breath of coming winter. The stars were brilliant and hung low in the frosty air. Looking at them, Laura sang the anthem again:

'The heavens declare the glory of God and
The Firmament showeth His handiwork.
Day unto day uttereth speech, and
Night unto night showeth knowledge.
There is no speech nor language
Where their voice is not heard.'

There was no sound but the soft clip-clop of Barnum's feet as he walked along the grassy prairie road.

'Sing the starlight song,' Almanzo asked, and Laura sang again, softly:

'In the starlight, in the starlight,
At the daylight's dewy close,
When the nightingale is singing
His last love song to the rose;
In the calm clear night of summer
When the breezes softly play,
From the glitter of our dwelling
We will softly steal away.
Where the silv'ry waters murmur
By the margin of the sea,
In the starlight, in the starlight,
We will wander gay and free.'

Again silence came and was unbroken while Barnum of his own accord turned north towards the house. Then Laura said, 'I've sung for you, now I'll give you a penny for your thoughts.'

'I was wondering . . .' Almanzo paused. Then he picked up Laura's hand that shone white in the starlight, and his sun-browned hand closed gently over it. He had never done that before. 'Your hand is so small,' he said. Another pause. Then quickly, 'I was wondering if you would like an engagement ring.'

'That would depend on who offered it to me,' Laura told him.

'If I should?' Almanzo asked.

'Then it would depend on the ring,' Laura answered, and drew her hand away.

It was later than usual when Almanzo came next Sunday.

'Sorry to be so late,' he said, when Laura was settled in the buggy and they were driving away.

'We can take a shorter drive,' Laura answered.

'But we want to go to Lake Henry. This is about our last chance for wild grapes, now they are frosted,' Almanzo told her.

It was a sunny afternoon, warm for the time of year. On either side of the narrow road between the twin lakes, ripened wild grapes were hanging from their vines in the trees. Almanzo drove slowly, and reaching from the buggy he and Laura picked the clusters of grapes. They ate of their tangy sweetness as they watched the water rippling in the sunshine and heard the little waves lapping on the shore.

As they drove home the sun went down in a flaming western sky. Twilight settled over the prairie, and the evening wind blew softly through the buggy.

Then driving with one hand, with the other Almanzo lifted Laura's, and she felt something cool slip over her third finger while he reminded her, 'You said it would depend on the ring. How do you like this one?'

Laura held her hand up to the first light of the new moon. The gold of the ring and its flat oval setting shone in the faint moon radiance. Three small stones set in the golden oval glimmered.

'The set is a garnet, with a pearl on each side,' Almanzo told her.

'It is a beautiful ring,' Laura said. 'I think . . . I would like to have it.'

'Then leave it on. It is yours and next summer I will build a little house in the grove on the tree claim. It will have to be a little house. Do you mind?'

'I have always lived in little houses. I like them,' Laura answered.

They had almost reached home. Lamplight shone from its windows and Pa was playing the fiddle. Laura knew the song, it was one that he often sang to Ma. His voice rose with its music and he sang:

> 'A beautiful castle I've built for thee
> In dreamland far away,
> And there, gentle darling, come dwell with
>   me,
> Where love alone has sway.
> Oh, sweet will be our blisses,
> Oh, rare will be our blisses!

We'll tell our time by the lovers' chime
That strikes the hour with kisses.'

Barnum was quiet while Laura and Almanzo stood beside the buggy when Pa's song was finished. Then Laura held up her face in the faint moonlight. 'You may kiss me good night,' she said, and after their first kiss she went into the house while Almanzo drove away.

Pa laid down his fiddle when Laura came in. He looked at her hand where the ring sparkled in the lamplight.

'I see it is settled,' he said. 'Almanzo was talking to me yesterday and I guess it's all right.'

'If only you are sure, Laura,' Ma said gently. 'Sometimes I think it is the horses you care for, more than their master.'

'I couldn't have one without the other,' Laura answered shakily.

Then Ma smiled at her, Pa cleared his throat gruffly, and Laura knew they understood what she was too shy to say.

24

Almanzo Goes Away

E ven at home Laura felt that her ring was conspicuous. Its smooth clasp was strange on her third finger, and the garnet and pearls were constantly catching the light. Several times on the way to school next morning she almost took it off and tied it into her handkerchief for safekeeping. But, after all, she was engaged; that could not always be a secret.

She did not mind being almost late to school that morning. There was barely time to slide into her seat with Ida before Mr Owen called the room to order, and quickly she opened a book so that it hid her left hand. But just as she was beginning to study, a glitter caught her eye.

Ida's left hand was resting on the desk where Laura would be sure to see the broad circlet of gold shining on the third finger.

Laura looked from the ring to Ida's laughing, blushing face and shy eyes, and then she broke a school rule. She whispered, 'Elmer?' Ida blushed even rosier, and nodded. Then under the edge of the desk, Laura showed Ida her own left hand.

Mary Power and Florence and Minnie could hardly wait until recess to pounce upon them and admire their rings. 'But I'm sorry you have them,' Mary Power said, 'for I suppose both of you will be quitting school now.'

'Not me,' Ida denied. 'I am going to school this winter, anyway.'

'So am I,' said Laura. 'I want to get a certificate again in the spring.'

'Will you teach school next summer?' Florence asked.

'If I can get a school,' Laura replied.

'I can get the school in our district if I can get a certificate,' Florence told them, 'but I'm afraid of teachers' examinations.'

'Oh, you will pass,' Laura encouraged her. 'There's nothing much to it, if only you don't get confused and forget what you know.'

'Well, I'm not engaged, nor do I want to teach,' said Mary Power. 'How about you, Ida? Are you going to teach for a while?'

Ida laughed, 'No, indeed! I never did want to teach. I'd rather keep house. Why do you suppose I got this ring?'

They all laughed with her, and Minnie asked, 'Well, why did you get yours, Laura? Don't you want to keep house?'

'Oh, yes,' Laura answered. 'But Almanzo has to build it first.' Then the big new bell clanged in the cupola, and recess was over.

There was no singing school now, so Laura did not expect to see Almanzo until the next Sunday. She was surprised when Pa asked her, Wednesday night, whether she had seen Almanzo.

'I saw him at the blacksmith shop,' Pa told her. 'He said he'd see you after school if he could, and if not, to tell you he didn't have time. It seems he and Royal are leaving next Sunday for Minnesota. Something's come up, and Royal's got to go sooner than he expected.'

Laura was shocked. She had known that Almanzo and his brother planned to spend the winter with their folks in Minnesota, but he had not intended to go so soon. It was shocking that the whole pattern of the days could be broken so suddenly. There would be no more Sunday drives.

'It may be best,' she said. 'They will be sure to reach Minnesota before snow falls.'

'Yes, they'll likely have good weather for the trip,' Pa agreed. 'I told him I'd keep Lady while they're gone. He's going to leave the buggy here, and he said you are to drive Lady as much as you please, Laura.'

'Oh, Laura! will you take me driving?' Carrie asked, and Grace cried, 'Me, too, Laura! Me, too?'

Laura promised that she would, but the rest of that week seemed oddly empty. She had not realized before how often, during a week, she had looked forward to the Sunday drives.

Early next Sunday morning, Almanzo and his brother Royal came. Royal was driving his own team, hitched to his pedlar's cart. Almanzo drove Lady, hitched single to his shining, lazy-back buggy. Pa came out of the stable to meet them, and Almanzo drove the buggy under the hay-covered shed. There he unhitched Lady, then led her into the stable.

Afterwards, leaving Pa and Royal talking, he came to the kitchen door. He hadn't time to stop, he told Ma, but he would like to see Laura for a moment.

Ma sent him into the sitting room, and as Laura turned from plumping up the cushions on the window seat, the ring on her hand sparkled in the morning light.

Almanzo smiled. 'Your new ring is becoming to your hand,' he said.

Laura turned her hand in the sunshine. The gold of the ring gleamed, the garnet glowed richly in the centre of the flat, oval set, and on either side of it the pearls shimmered lustrously.

'It is beautiful, this ring,' she said.

'I would say the hand,' Almanzo replied. Then, 'I suppose your father told you that Royal and I are going home sooner than we expected. Royal decided to drive through Iowa, so we are starting now. I brought Lady and the buggy over, for you to use whenever you please.'

'Where is Prince?' Laura asked.

'One of my neighbours is keeping Prince, and Lady's colt, and Cap is keeping Barnum and Skip. I'll need all four of them in the spring.' A shrill whistle sounded from outside, 'Royal is calling, so kiss me good-bye and I'll go,' Almanzo finished.

They kissed quickly, then Laura went with him to the door and watched while he and Royal drove away. She felt left behind and unhappy. Then at her elbow Carrie asked, 'Are you going to be lonesome?' so soberly that Laura smiled.

'No, I'm not going to be lonesome,' she answered stoutly. 'After dinner we will hitch up Lady and go for a drive.'

Pa came in and went to the stove. 'It's getting so a fire feels good,' he said. 'Caroline, what would you think of staying here all winter, instead of going to town? I've been figuring. I believe I can rent the building in town this winter, and if I can, I can tar paper and side this house. Maybe even paint it.'

'That would be a gain, Charles,' Ma said at once.

'Another thing,' Pa continued. 'We have so much stock now, it would be a big job to move all the hay and fodder. With this house sided outside, and good thick building paper inside, we'd be snug here. We can put up the coal heater in the sitting room and get our winter's supply of coal. There's a cellarful of vegetables from the garden, pumpkins and squashes from the field. Even if the winter's so bad I can't get to town often, we won't need to worry about being hungry or cold.'

'That is true,' said Ma. 'But, Charles, the girls must go to school, and it's too far for them to walk in the wintertime. A blizzard might come up.'

'I will drive them there and back,' Pa promised. 'It's only a mile, and it will be a quick trip with the bobsled and no load.'

'Very well,' Ma consented. 'If you rent the building in town, and want to stay here, I am satisfied to do so. I will be glad not to move.'

So before snow fell, all was snug on the homestead claim. In its new siding the little house was really a house, no longer a claim shanty. Inside, thick grey building paper covered all the pineboard walls. They had grown so brown with time, that the lighter paper brightened the rooms, and the freshly starched white muslin curtains gave them a crisp look.

When the first heavy snows came, Pa put the wagon box on the bobsled runners, and half-filled it with hay. Then on school days, Laura and Carrie, with Grace snuggled between them, sat on the blanket-covered hay, with other blankets tucked over and around them, while Pa drove them to the schoolhouse in the morning and brought them home at night to the warmly welcoming house.

Every afternoon on his way to the school, he stopped at the post office, and once or twice a week there was a letter for Laura, from Almanzo. He had reached his father's home in Minnesota; he would come back in the spring.

25

The Night Before Christmas

On Christmas Eve again, there was a Christmas tree at the church in town. In good time, the Christmas box had gone to Mary, and the house was full of Christmas secrets as the girls hid from each other to wrap the presents for the Christmas tree. But at ten o'clock that morning, snow began to fall.

Still it seemed that it might be possible to go to the Christmas tree. All the afternoon Grace watched from the window, and once or twice the wind moderated. By suppertime, however, it was howling at the eaves, and the air was thick with flying snow.

'It's too dangerous to risk it,' Pa said. It was a straight wind, blowing steadily, but you never could tell; it might turn into a blizzard while the people were in the church.

No plans had been made for Christmas Eve at home, so everyone had much to do. In the kitchen Laura was popping corn in the iron kettle set into a hole of the stove top from which she had removed the stove lid. She put a handful of salt into the kettle; when it was hot she put in a handful of popcorn. With a long-handled spoon she stirred it, while with the other hand she held the kettle's cover to keep the corn from flying out as it popped. When it stopped popping she dropped in another handful of corn and kept on stirring, but now she need not hold the cover, for the popped white kernels stayed on top and kept the popping kernels from jumping out of the kettle.

Ma was boiling molasses in a pan. When Laura's kettle was full of popped corn, Ma dipped some into a large pan, poured a thin trickle of the boiling molasses over it, and then buttering her hands, she deftly squeezed handfuls of it into popcorn balls. Laura kept popping corn and Ma made it into balls until the large dishpan was heaped with their sweet crispness.

In the sitting room Carrie and Grace made little bags of pink mosquito netting, left over last summer from the screen door. They filled the bags with Christmas candy that Pa had brought from town that week.

'It's lucky I thought we'd want more candy than we'd likely get at the Christmas tree,' Pa took credit to himself.

'Oh!' Carrie discovered. 'We've made one bag too many. Grace miscounted.'

'I did not!' Grace cried.

'Grace,' Ma said.

'I am not contradicting!' cried Grace.

'Grace,' said Pa.

Grace gulped. 'Pa,' she said. 'I didn't count wrong. I guess I can count five! There was candy enough for another one, and it looks pretty in the pink bag.'

'So it does, and it is nice to have an extra one. We haven't always been so lucky,' Pa told her.

Laura remembered the Christmas on the Verdigris River in Indian Territory, when Mr Edwards had walked eighty miles to bring her and Mary each one stick of candy. Wherever he was tonight, she wished him as much happiness as he had brought them. She remembered the Christmas Eve on Plum Creek in Minnesota, when Pa had been lost in the blizzard and they feared he would never come back. He had eaten the Christmas candy while he lay sheltered three days under the creek bank. Now here they were, in the snug warm house, with plenty of candy and other good things.

Yet now she wished that Mary was there, and she was trying not to think of Almanzo. When he first went away, letters had come from him often; then they had come regularly. Now for three weeks there had been no letter. He was at home, Laura thought, meeting his old friends and the girls he used to know. Springtime was four months away. He might forget her, or wish that he had not given her the ring that sparkled on her finger.

Pa broke into her thoughts. 'Bring me the fiddle, Laura. Let's have a little music before we begin on these good things.'

She brought him the fiddle box and he tuned the fiddle and resined the bow. 'What shall I play?'

'Play Mary's song first,' Laura answered. 'Perhaps she is thinking of us.'

Pa drew the bow across the strings and he and the fiddle sang:

> 'Ye banks and braes and streams around
> The castle of Montgomery,
> Green be your woods and fair your flowers,
> Your waters never drumlie;
> There summer first unfolds her robes
> And there the langest tarry,
> For there I took the last fareweel
> Of my sweet Highland Mary.'

One Scots song reminded Pa of another, and with the fiddle he sang:

> 'My heart is sair, I dare na tell,
> My heart is sair for somebody.
> Oh! I could wake a winter night,
> A' for the sake o' somebody.'

Ma sat in her rocking chair beside the heater, and Carrie and Grace were snug in the window seat, but Laura moved restlessly around the room.

The fiddle sang a wandering tune of its own that made her remember June's wild roses. Then it caught up another tune to blend with Pa's voice.

> 'When marshalled on the mighty plane,
> The glittering hosts bestud the sky
> One star alone of all the train
> Can catch the sinner's wandering eye.
> It was my light, my guide, my all,
> It bade my dark forebodings cease,
> And through the storm and dangers thrall
> It led me to the port of peace.
> Now safely moored, my perils o'er,
> I'll sing, first in night's diadem
> Forever and forever more,
> The Star – the Star of Bethlehem.'

Grace said softly, 'The Christmas star.'

The fiddle sang to itself again while Pa cocked his head, listening. 'The wind is rising,' he said. 'Good thing we stayed home.'

Then the fiddle began to laugh and Pa's voice laughed as he sang:

> 'Oh, do not stand so long outside,
> Why need you be so shy?
> The people's ears are open, John,

As they are passing by!
You can not tell what they may think,
They've said strange things before
And if you wish to talk awhile,
Come in and shut the door!
Come in! Come in! Come in!'

Laura looked at Pa in amazement as he sang so loudly, looking at the door. 'Come in! Come in! Come . . .'

Someone knocked at the door. Pa nodded to Laura to go to the door, while he ended the song. 'Come in and shut the door!'

A gust of wind swirled snow into the room when Laura opened the door; it blinded her for a moment and when she could see she could not believe her eyes. The wind whirled snow around Almanzo as, speechless, she stood holding the door open.

'Come in!' Pa called. 'Come in and shut the door!' Shivering, he laid the fiddle in its box and put more coal on the fire. 'That wind blows the cold into a fellow's bones,' he said. 'What about your team?'

'I drove Prince, and I put him in the stable beside Lady,' Almanzo answered, as he shook the snow from his overcoat and hung it with his cap on the polished buffalo horns fastened to the wall near the door, while Ma rose from her chair to greet him.

Laura had retreated to the other end of the room,

beside Carrie and Grace. When Almanzo looked towards them, Grace said, 'I made an extra bag of candy.'

'And I brought some oranges,' Almanzo answered, taking a paper bag from his overcoat pocket. 'I have a package with Laura's name on it, too, but isn't she going to speak to me?'

'I can't believe it is you,' Laura murmured. 'You said you would be gone all winter.'

'I decided I didn't want to stay away so long, and as you will speak to me, here is your Christmas gift.'

'Come, Charles, put the fiddle away,' said Ma. 'Carrie and Grace, help me bring in the popcorn balls.'

Laura opened the small package that Almanzo gave her. The white paper unfolded; there was a white box inside. She lifted its lid. There in a nest of soft white cotton lay a gold bar brooch. On its surface was etched a little house, and before it along the bar lay a tiny lake, and a spray of grasses and leaves.

'Oh, it's beautiful,' she breathed. 'Thank you!'

'Can't you thank a fellow better than that?' he asked, and then he put his arms around her while Laura kissed him and whispered, 'I am glad you came back.'

Pa came from the kitchen bringing a hodful of coal and Ma followed. Carrie brought in the pan of popcorn balls and Grace gave everyone a bag of candy.

While they ate the sweets, Almanzo told of driving all day in the cold winds and camping on the open prairie with no house nor shelter near, as he and Royal drove south into Nebraska. He told of seeing the beautiful capital building at Omaha; of muddy roads when they turned east into Iowa, where the farmers were burning their corn for fuel because they could not sell it for as much as twenty-five cents a bushel. He told of seeing the Iowa state capital at Des Moines; of rivers in flood that they crossed in Iowa and Missouri, until when faced with the Missouri River they turned north again.

So with interesting talk the evening sped by until the old clock struck twelve.

'Merry Christmas!' Ma said, rising from her chair, and 'Merry Christmas!' everyone answered.

Almanzo put on his overcoat, his cap and mittens, said good night, and went out into the storm. Faintly the sleigh bells rang as he passed the house on his way home.

'Did you hear them before?' Laura asked Pa.

'Yes, and nobody was ever asked to come in oftener than he was,' said Pa. 'I suppose he couldn't hear me in the storm.'

'Come, come, girls,' Ma said. 'If you don't get to sleep soon, Santa Claus will have no chance to fill the stockings.'

In the morning, there would be all the surprises from the stockings, and at noon there would be the special Christmas feast, with a big fat hen stuffed and roasted, brown and juicy, and Almanzo would be there, for Ma had asked him to Christmas dinner. The wind was blowing hard, but it had not the shriek and howl of a blizzard wind, so probably he would be able to come tomorrow.

'Oh, Laura!' Carrie said, as Laura blew out the lamp in the bedroom. 'Isn't this the nicest Christmas! Do Christmases get better all the time?'

'Yes,' Laura said. 'They do.'

26

Teachers' Examinations

Through a March snowstorm Laura rode to town with Pa in the bobsled, to take the teachers' examinations. There was no school that day, so Carrie and Grace stayed at home.

Winter had been pleasant on the claim, but Laura was glad that spring was coming soon. Vaguely, as she rode in the nest of blankets on the hay, she thought of the pleasant winter Sundays with the family and Almanzo in the cosy sitting room, and she looked forward to long drives again through the summer sunshine and wind; she wondered if Barnum would still be gentle after the long winter in a stable.

As they neared the schoolhouse, Pa asked if she were nervous about the examinations.

'Oh, no,' she answered through the frosty veil. 'I am sure I can pass. I wish I were as sure of getting a school I will like.'

'You could have the Perry school again,' said Pa.

'I would rather have a larger one with more pay,' Laura explained.

'Well,' Pa said cheerfully as they stopped at the school-house, 'the first bridge is the examinations, and here we are! Time enough to cross the next bridge when we come to it.'

Laura was impatient with herself because she felt timid when she went into the room full of strangers. Nearly every desk was occupied, and the only person she knew was Florence Wilkins. When she touched Florence's hand, she was startled; it was cold as ice, and Florence's lips were pale from nervousness. Laura felt so sorry for her that she forgot her own timidity.

'I'm scared,' Florence said in a low, shaking voice. 'All the others are old teachers, and the examination is going to be hard. I know I'll never pass.'

'Pooh! I bet they're scared, too!' Laura said. 'Don't worry; you'll pass all right. Just don't be frightened. You know you've always passed examinations.'

Then the bell rang, and Laura faced the lists of questions. Florence was right; they were hard. Working her way through them, Laura was tired when intermission came. By noon she felt her own heart failing; she began to fear she would not get a certificate, but she worked doggedly on until at last she was through. Her last paper was collected with the others, and Pa came to take her home.

'I don't know, Pa,' she said in answer to his question. 'It was harder than I expected, but I did the best I could.'

'No one can do better than that,' Pa assured her.

At home, Ma said that no doubt it would be all right.

'Now don't fret! Forget about it until you hear the results of the examinations.'

Ma's advice was always good, but Laura repeated it to herself every day and almost every hour. She went to sleep telling herself; 'Don't worry,' and woke up thinking with dread: The letter may come today.

At school, Florence had no hope for either of them. 'It was too hard,' she said. 'I'm sure only a few of the oldest teachers passed it.'

A week went by, with no word. Laura hardly expected Almanzo to come that Sunday, for Royal was sick with influenza. Almanzo did not come. There was no letter on Monday. There was no letter on Tuesday.

A warm wind had melted the snow to slush and the sun was shining, so on Wednesday Pa did not come for Laura. She and Carrie and Grace walked home. The letter was there; Pa had got it that morning.

'What does it say, Ma?' Laura cried as she dropped her coat and crossed the room to pick up the letter.

'Why, Laura!' Ma said in astonishment. 'You know I'd no more look at another person's letter than I'd steal.'

With shaking fingers Laura tore the envelope and took out a teacher's certificate. It was a second-grade one.

'It's better than I expected,' she told Ma. 'The most I hoped for was third grade. Now if I can only have the good luck to get the right school!'

'A body makes his own luck, be it good or bad,' Ma

placidly said. 'I have no doubt you will get as good as you deserve.'

Laura had no doubt that she would get as good a school as she could get, but she wondered how to make herself the good luck to get the one she wanted. She thought about little else that night, and she was still thinking about it next morning when Florence came into the schoolroom and came directly to her.

'Did you pass, Laura?' she asked.

'Yes, I got a second-grade certificate,' Laura answered.

'I didn't get any, so I can't teach our school,' Florence said soberly, 'but this is what I want to tell you: You tried to help me, and I would rather you taught our school than anyone else. If you want it, my father says you may have it. It is a three months' school, beginning the first of April, and it pays thirty dollars a month.'

Laura could hardly get the breath to answer, 'Oh, yes! I do want it.'

'Father said, if you did, to come and see him and the board will sign the contract.'

'I will be there tomorrow afternoon,' Laura said. 'Thank you, Florence, *so* much.'

'Well, you have always been so nice to me, I am glad of a chance to pay some of it back,' Florence told her.

Laura remembered what Ma had said about luck, and she thought to herself: 'I believe we make most of our luck without intending to.'

27

School Days End

At the end of the last day of school in March, Laura gathered her books, and stacked them neatly on her slate. She looked around the schoolroom for the last time. She would never come back. Monday she would begin teaching the Wilkins school, and sometime next fall she and Almanzo would be married.

Carrie and Grace were waiting downstairs, but Laura lingered at her desk, feeling a strange sinking of heart. Ida and Mary Power and Florence would be here next week. Carrie and Grace would walk to school without her, always after this.

Except for Mr Owen at his desk, the room was empty now. Laura must go. She picked up her books and went towards the door. At Mr Owen's desk she stopped and said, 'I must bid you good-bye, for I shall not be coming back.'

'I heard you were going to teach again,' Mr Owen said. 'We will miss you, but we will look for you back next fall.'

'That is what I want to tell you. This is good-bye,' Laura repeated. 'I am going to be married, so I won't be coming back at all.'

Mr Owen sprang up and walked nervously across the platform and back. 'I'm sorry,' he said. 'Not sorry you are going to be married, but sorry I didn't graduate you this spring. I held you back because I . . . because I had a foolish pride; I wanted to graduate the whole class together, and some weren't ready. It was not fair to you. I'm sorry.'

'It doesn't matter,' Laura said. 'I am glad to know I could have graduated.'

Then they shook hands, and Mr Owen said good-bye and wished her good fortune in all her undertakings.

As Laura went down the stairs she thought: 'The last time always seems sad, but it isn't really. The end of one thing is only the beginning of another.'

After Sunday night supper at home, Almanzo and Laura drove through town and northwest towards the Wilkins' claim. It was three and a half miles from town, and Barnum walked. The twilight deepened into night. Stars came out in the vastness of the sky and the prairie stretched dim and mysterious far away. The buggy wheels turned softly on the grassy road.

In the stillness Laura began to sing:

'The stars are rolling in the sky,
The earth rolls on below,
And we can feel the rattling wheel
Revolving as we go;
Then tread away my gallant boys,

239

And make the axle fly!
Why should not wheels go round-about,
Like planets in the sky?'

Almanzo laughed aloud. 'Your songs are like your father's! They always fit.'

'That is from the "Old Song of the Treadmill",' Laura told him. 'But it did seem to fit the stars and buggy wheels.'

'There's only one word wrong in it,' Almanzo agreed. 'No buggy wheels of mine will ever rattle. I keep 'em tight and greased. But never mind. When the wheels roll around in this direction for three months more, you will be through teaching school, for good!'

'I suppose you mean, for better or worse,' Laura said demurely. 'But it better be for good.'

'It will be,' Almanzo said.

28

The Cream-coloured Hat

The new schoolhouse stood on a corner of Mr Wilkins' claim, only a little way from his house. When Laura opened its door on Monday morning, she saw that it was an exact replica of the Perry schoolhouse, even to the dictionary on the desk, and the nail in the wall for her sunbonnet.

This was a happy omen, she thought; and it was. All her days in that school were pleasant. She felt herself a capable teacher now, and she dealt so well with every little difficulty that none ever lasted until the next day. Her pupils were friendly and obedient, and the little ones were often funny, though she kept her smiles unseen.

She boarded at the Wilkins', and they were all friendly to Laura and pleasant to each other. Florence still went to school and at night told Laura all the day's happenings. Laura shared Florence's room, and they spent the evenings cosily there with their books.

On the last Friday in April, Mr Wilkins paid Laura twenty-two dollars, her first month's salary, less two dollars a week for her board. Almanzo drove her home that evening, and next day she went with Ma to town to buy materials. They bought bleached muslin for underwear, chemises and drawers, petticoats and nightgowns; two of each. 'These, with what you have, should be plenty,' said Ma. They bought stronger, but bleached muslin, for two pairs of sheets and two pairs of pillow cases.

For Laura's summer dress they bought ten yards of delicate pink lawn with small flowers and pale green leaves scattered over it. Then they went to Miss Bell's to find a hat to go with the dress.

There were several beautiful hats, but Laura knew at once which one she wanted. It was a fine, cream-coloured straw with a narrow brim, rolled narrower at the sides. The brim in front came down over the middle of Laura's forehead. Around the crown was a band of satin ribbon a little darker than the straw, and three ostrich tips stood straight up at the crown's left side. They were shaded in colour, from the light cream of the straw to slightly darker than the satin ribbon. The hat was held on the head by a fine, white silk elastic cord that scarcely showed because it fitted under the mass of Laura's plaited hair.

As they walked up the street after they had bought that hat, Laura begged Ma to take five dollars and spend it for herself.

'No, Laura,' Ma refused. 'You are a good girl to think of it, but there is nothing that I need.'

So they came to the wagon, waiting for them in front

of Fuller's hardware store. Something bulky stood in the wagon box, covered with a horse blanket. Laura wondered what it was, but she had no time to look, for Pa untied the horses quickly and they all started home.

'What have you got, Charles?' Ma asked.

'I can't show you now, Caroline. Wait until we get home,' Pa answered.

At home he stopped the wagon close to the house door. 'Now, girls,' he said, 'take your own packages in, but leave mine alone until I get back from putting up the horses. Don't you peek under the blanket either!'

He unhitched the horses and hurried them away.

'Now whatever can that be?' Ma said to Laura. They waited. As soon as possible, Pa came hurrying back. He lifted the blanket away, and there stood a shining new sewing machine.

'Oh, Charles!' Ma gasped.

'Yes, Caroline, it is yours,' Pa said proudly. 'There'll be a lot of extra sewing, with Mary coming home and Laura going away, and I thought you'd need some help.'

'But how could you?' Ma asked, touching the shiny black iron of the machine's legs.

'I had to sell a cow anyway, Caroline; there wouldn't be room in the stable next winter unless I did,' Pa explained. 'Now if you will help me unload this thing, we will take its cover off and see how it looks.'

A long time ago, Laura remembered, a tone in Ma's

voice when she spoke of a sewing machine had made Laura think that she wanted one. Pa had remembered that.

He took the endgate out of the wagon, and he and Ma and Laura lifted the sewing machine carefully down and carried it into the sitting room, while Carrie and Grace hovered around excitedly. Then Pa lifted the box-cover of the machine and they stood in silent admiration.

'It is beautiful,' Ma said at last, 'and what a help it will be. I can hardly wait to use it.' But this was late on Saturday afternoon. The sewing machine must stand still over Sunday.

Next week Ma studied the instruction book and learned to run the machine, and the next Saturday she and Laura began to work on the lawn dress. The lawn was so crisp and fresh, the colours so dainty, that Laura was afraid to cut it lest she make a mistake, but Ma had made so many dresses that she did not hesitate. She took Laura's measurements; then, with her dressmaker chart, she made the pattern for the bodice, and fearlessly cut the lawn.

They made the bodice tight-fitting, with two clusters of tucks down the back, and two in front. Down the centre of the front, between the tucks, tiny, white pearl buttons buttoned the dress. The collar was a straight, upstanding fold of the lawn; the sleeves were long, gathered at the shoulders, and close-fitting to the wrist, finished with a hem the width of the tucks.

The skirt was gathered very full all round into a narrow waistband, which buttoned over the bottom of the bodice to secure them from slipping apart. All down the full skirt, tucks went around and around it, spaced evenly a little way apart, and beneath the bottom tuck was a full-gathered ruffle four inches wide that just touched Laura's shoe tips.

This dress was finished when Almanzo brought Laura home on the last Friday in May.

'Oh! it is pretty, Ma!' Laura said when she saw it. 'All those tucks are so even, and stitched so beautifully.'

'I declare,' said Ma. 'I don't know how we ever got along without that sewing machine. It does the work so easily; tucking is no trouble at all. And such beautiful stitching. The best of seamstresses could not possibly equal it by hand.'

Laura was silent a moment, looking at her new, machine-stitched dress. Then she said, 'Mr Wilkins paid me another month's salary today, and I really don't need it. I have fifteen dollars left of my April pay. I will need a new dress for next fall . . .'

'Yes, and you will need a nice wedding dress,' Ma interrupted.

'Fifteen dollars ought to buy the two,' Laura considered. 'They, with the clothes I have, will be enough for a long time. Besides, I will have another twenty-two dollars next month. I wish you and Pa would take this fifteen dollars. Please, Ma. Use it to pay for Mary's visit home, or to buy the clothes she needs.'

'We can manage without taking the money for your last term of school,' Ma said quietly.

'I know you can, but there are so many things for you and Pa to manage. I would like to help again just this once. Then I would feel all right about going away and not helping any more, and having all these nice clothes for myself,' Laura urged.

Ma yielded. 'If it will please you to do so, give the money to your Pa. Since he spent the cow money for the sewing machine, he will be glad to have it, I know.'

Pa was surprised and objected that Laura would need the money herself. But when she explained and urged again, he took it gladly. 'It will help me out of a pinch,' he admitted. 'But this is the last one. From now on I think we will have clear sailing. The town is growing so fast that I am going to have plenty of carpenter work. The cattle are growing fast, too. Beats all how they multiply, and they live off the homestead, and next year I win my bet with Uncle Sam and this homestead will be ours. So you need never worry about helping any more, Half-Pint. You have done your share and then some.'

When she drove away with Almanzo that Sunday evening, Laura's heart was brimming with contentment. But it seemed that always there must be some wish unsatisfied. Now she regretted that she would miss Mary's coming home. Mary was coming that week, and Laura would be teaching a class fractions in Wilkins' school when Mary came.

On Friday afternoon, Almanzo drove Prince and Lady, and they trotted fast all the way home. As they came near the door of home, Laura heard the music of the organ. Before Almanzo stopped the horses she was out of the buggy and running into the house.

'See you Sunday,' he called after her, and she fluttered her ringed hand in answer. Then she was giving Mary a big hug before she could get up from the organ stool, and the first thing Mary said was, 'Oh, Laura! I was so surprised to find the organ waiting here for me.'

'We had to keep the secret a long time,' Laura answered. 'But it didn't spoil by keeping, did it? Oh, Mary, let me look at you. How well you're looking!'

Mary was even more beautiful than ever. Laura would never grow tired of looking at her. And now there was so much to tell each other that they talked every moment. Sunday afternoon they walked once more to the top of the low hill beyond the stable, and Laura picked wild roses to fill Mary's arms.

'Laura,' Mary asked soberly, 'do you really want to leave home to marry that Wilder boy?'

Laura was serious too. 'He isn't that Wilder boy any more, Mary. He is Almanzo. You don't know anything about him, do you? or not much since the Hard Winter.'

'I remember his going after the wheat, of course. But why do you want to leave home and go with him?' Mary persisted.

'I guess it's because we just seem to belong together,' Laura said. 'Besides, I have practically left home anyway; I am away so much. I won't be any farther away than I am at Wilkins'.'

'Oh, well, I guess it has to be that way. I went away to college, and now you're going away. That's growing up, I suppose.'

'It's strange to think,' Laura said. 'Carrie and Grace are

older now than we used to be. They are growing up, too. Yet it would be even stranger if we stayed as we were for always, wouldn't it?'

'There he is coming now,' said Mary. She had heard the buggy and Prince's and Lady's hoofs, and no one could have guessed that she was blind, to see her beautiful blue eyes turned towards them as if she saw them. 'I've hardly seen you,' she said. 'And now you have to go.'

'Not till after supper. I'll be back next Friday, and besides, we'll have all July and most of August together,' Laura reminded her.

At four o'clock on the last Friday in June, Almanzo drove Barnum and Skip up to the Wilkins' door to take Laura home. As they drove along the familiar road, he said, 'And so another school is finished, the last one.'

'Are you sure?' Laura replied demurely.

'Aren't we?' he asked. 'You will be frying my breakfast pancakes sometime along the last of September.'

'Or maybe a little later,' Laura promised. He had already begun to build the house on the tree claim.

'In the meantime, how about the Fourth of July? Do you want to go to the celebration?'

'I'd much rather go for a drive,' Laura answered.

'Suits me!' he agreed. 'This team's getting too frisky again. I've been working on the house and they've had a few days' rest. It's time we took the ginger out of them on some more of those long drives.'

'Any time! I'm free now.' Laura was gay. She felt like a bird out of a cage.

'We'll have the first long drive on the Fourth, then,' said Almanzo.

So on the Fourth, soon after dinner, Laura put on her new lawn dress for the first time, and for the first time she wore the cream-coloured hat with the shaded ostrich tips. She was ready when Almanzo came.

Barnum and Skip stood for her to get into the buggy, but they were nervous and in a hurry to go. 'The crowd excited them, coming through town,' Almanzo said. 'We will only go to the end of Main Street, where you can see the flags, then we will go south, away from the noise.'

The road south towards Brewster's was so changed that it hardly seemed to be the same road that they had travelled so many times to Laura's first school. New claim shanties and some houses were scattered over the prairie, and there were many fields of growing grain. Cattle and horses were feeding along the way.

Instead of being white with blowing snow, the prairie was many shades of soft green, but the wind still blew. It came from the south and was warm; it blew the wild grass and the grain in the fields; it blew the horses' manes and tails streaming behind them; it blew the fringes of the lap robe that was tucked in tightly to protect Laura's delicate lawn dress. And it blew the lovely, cream-coloured ostrich feathers off Laura's hat.

She caught them with the very tips of her fingers as they were being whirled away. 'Oh! Oh!' she exclaimed in vexation. 'It must be they were not sewed on well.'

'Miss Bell hasn't been in the West long enough yet,' Almanzo said. 'She is not used to prairie winds. Better let me put those feathers in my pocket before you lose them.'

It was suppertime when they came home, and Almanzo stayed to help eat the cold remains of the Fourth of July dinner. There was plenty of cold chicken and pie; there was a cake and a pitcher of lemonade made with fresh, cold water from the well.

At supper Almanzo proposed that Carrie go with him and Laura to see the fireworks in town. 'The horses have had such a long drive that I think they will behave,' he said, but Ma replied, 'Of course Laura will go if she wishes; she is used to circus horses. But Carrie better not.' So Laura and Almanzo went.

They kept the horses well outside the crowd, so that no one would be trampled or run over. In an open space at a safe distance they sat in the buggy and waited until a streak of fire rose in the darkness above the crowd and exploded a star.

At the first flash Barnum reared and Skip leaped. They came down running, and the buggy came down and ran after them. Almanzo swung them in a wide circle, bringing them to face the fireworks again just as another star exploded.

'Don't bother about the horses,' he told Laura. 'I'll manage them. You watch the fireworks.'

So Laura did. After each explosion of beauty against the darkness, Almanzo drove the circle, always bringing Barnum and Skip around in time to face the next rush and blossom of fire. Not until the last shower of sparks had faded did Almanzo and Laura drive away.

Then Laura said, 'It is really a good thing that you have my feathers in your pocket. If they had been on my hat while I was watching the fireworks, they would have been twisted off, we whirled so fast.'

'Are they in my pocket yet?' Almanzo exclaimed in surprise.

'I hope so,' said Laura. 'If they are, I can sew them on my hat again.'

The feathers were still in his pocket, and as he handed them to her at home he said, 'I will be by for you Sunday. These horses do need exercise.'

29

Summer Storm

The heat was intense that week, and in church on Sunday morning Laura gasped for air. Shimmering heat waves quivered upward outside the windows, and the fitful little breezes were hot.

When church was over, Almanzo was waiting outside to take Laura home. As he helped her into the buggy he said, 'Your mother asked me to dinner, and afterwards we will exercise these horses again. It will be hot this afternoon,' he said in the buggy, 'but driving will be pleasanter than sitting in the house, if it doesn't storm.'

'My feathers are sewed on tight,' Laura laughed. 'So let the wind blow.'

Soon after Ma's good Sunday dinner, they set out, driving southward over the gently rolling, endless prairie. The sun shone fiercely, and even in the shade of the swiftly moving buggy top, the heat was oppressive. Instead of flowing smoothly and cool, the breeze came in warm puffs.

The shimmering heat-waves made a silvery appearance that retreated before them in the road ahead, like water, and phantom winds played in the grasses, twisting them in frantic writhings and passing on, up and away.

After a time, dark clouds began to gather in the northwest, and the heat grew still more intense.

'This is a queer afternoon. I think we'd better go home,' Almanzo said.

'Yes, let's do, and hurry,' Laura urged. 'I don't like the way the weather feels.'

The black mass of clouds was rising quickly as Almanzo turned the horses towards home. He stopped them and gave the reins to Laura. 'Hold them while I put on the buggy curtains. It's going to rain,' he said.

Quickly, behind the buggy, he unbuttoned the straps that held the top's back curtain rolled up. He let it unroll, and buttoned it at the sides and bottom, tightly closing in the back of the buggy. Then from under the seat he brought out the two side curtains, and buttoned them along their tops and sides to the sides of the buggy top, closing them in.

Then, back in his seat, he unrolled the rubber storm apron, and set the pleat in its bottom edge over the top of the dashboard, where it fitted snugly.

Laura admired the cleverness of this storm apron. There was a slot in it that fitted over the whipsocket, so the whip stood up in its place. There was a slit through which Almanzo passed the lines; he could hold them in his hands under the storm apron, and a flap fell over the slit to keep rain from coming in. The apron was so wide that it came down to the buggy box on either side, and it buttoned up to the side frames of the buggy top.

All this was done quickly. In a moment or two, Laura and Almanzo were snugly sheltered in a box of rubber curtains. No rain could come through the apron, the curtains, nor the buggy top overhead. Above the edge of the storm apron, that was as high as their chins, they could look out.

As Almanzo took the lines from Laura and started the horses, he said, 'Now let it rain!'

'Yes,' Laura said, 'if it must, but maybe we can beat the storm home.'

Almanzo was already urging the team. They went swiftly, but even more swiftly the black cloud rose, rolling and rumbling in the sky. Laura and Almanzo watched it in silence. The whole earth seemed silent and motionless in terror. The sound of the horses' fast-trotting feet and the tiny creaks of the speeding buggy seemed small in the stillness.

The swelling great mass of clouds writhed and wrestled, twisting together as if in fury and agony. Flickers of red lightning stabbed through them. Still the air was motionless and there was no sound. The heat increased. Laura's bangs were damp with perspiration, and uncurled on her forehead, while trickles ran down her cheeks and her neck. Almanzo urged on the horses.

Almost overhead now, the tumbling, swirling clouds

changed from black to a terrifying greenish-purple. They seemed to draw themselves together, then a groping finger slowly came out of them and stretched down, trying to reach the earth. It reached, and pulled itself up, and reached again.

'How far away is that?' Laura asked.

'Ten miles, I'd say,' Almanzo replied.

It was coming towards them, from the northwest, as they sped towards the northeast. No horses, however fast they ran, could outrun the speed of those clouds. Green-purple, they rolled in the sky above the helpless prairie, and reached towards it playfully as a cat's paw torments a mouse.

A second point came groping down, behind the first. Then another. All three reached and withdrew and reached again, down from the writhing clouds.

Then they all turned a little towards the south. One after another, quickly, all three points touched the earth, under the cloud-mass and travelling swiftly with it. They passed behind the buggy, to the west, and went on southward. A terrific wind blew suddenly, so strong that the buggy swayed, but the storm had passed. Laura drew a long, shaking breath.

'If we had been home, Pa would have sent us down cellar,' she said. 'And I would have been glad to go,' she added.

'We'd have needed a cellar, if that storm had come our

way. I never did run to a cyclone cellar, but if I ever meet a cloud like that, I will,' Almanzo admitted.

The wind abruptly changed. It blew from the southwest and brought a sudden cold with it.

'Hail,' Almanzo said.

'Yes,' said Laura. Somewhere, hail had fallen from that cloud.

Everyone at home was glad to see them. Laura had never seen Ma so pale, nor so thankful. Pa said that they had shown good judgement in turning back when they did. 'That storm is doing bad damage,' he said.

'It's a good idea, out here in this country, to have a cellar,' said Almanzo. He asked what Pa thought of their driving out across country, where the storm had passed, to see if anyone needed help. So Laura was left at home, while Pa and Almanzo drove away.

Though the storm was gone and the sky now clear, still they were nervous.

The afternoon passed, and Laura had changed into her weekday clothes and with Carrie's help had done the chores, before Pa and Almanzo came back. Ma set a cold supper on the table, and while they ate they told what they had seen in the path of the storm.

One settler not far south of town had just finished threshing his wheat crop from a hundred acres. It had been a splendid crop, that would have paid all his debts and left money in the bank. He and the threshers had been working that day to finish the job, and he was on a strawstack when they saw the storm coming.

He had just sent his two young boys to return a wagon he had borrowed from a neighbour to help in the threshing. He got into his cyclone cellar just in time. The storm carried away his grain, strawstacks and machinery, wagons, stables, and house; everything. Nothing was left but his bare claim.

The two boys on the mules had disappeared completely. But just before Pa and Almanzo reached the place, the older boy had come back, stark naked. He was nine years old. He said that he and his brother were riding the mules home, running, when the storm struck them. It lifted them all together and carried them around in a circle, in the air, still harnessed together side by side. They were whirled around, faster and faster and higher, until he began to get dizzy and he shouted to his little brother to hold on tight to his mule. Just then the air filled thickly with whirling straw and darkened so that he could see nothing. He felt a jerk of the harness breaking apart, and then he must have fainted. For the next thing he knew, he was alone in clear air.

He could see the ground beneath him. He was being carried around in a circle, all the time sinking a little, until finally he was not far above the earth. He tried to spring up, to get his feet under him, then struck the ground running, ran a little way, and fell. After lying there a few moments to rest, he got up and made his way home.

He had come to the ground a little more than a mile from his father's claim. There was not a shred of clothing left on him; even his high, laced boots had disappeared, but he was not hurt at all. It was a mystery how his boots had been taken from his feet without so much as bruising them.

Neighbours were searching far and wide for the other boy and the mules, but not a trace could be found of them. There could be hardly a hope that they were alive.

'Still, if that door came through,' Almanzo said.

'What door?' Carrie wanted to know.

That was the strangest thing that Pa and Almanzo had seen that day. It happened at another settler's claim, farther south. Everything had been stripped clean off his place, too. When this man and his family came up from their cyclone cellar, two bare spots were all that were left of stable and house. Oxen, wagon, tools, chickens, everything was gone. They had nothing but the clothes they wore, and one quilt that his wife had snatched to wrap around the baby in the cellar.

This man said to Pa, 'I'm a lucky man; I didn't have a crop to lose.' They had moved on to their claim only that spring, and he had been able to put in only a few sod potatoes.

That afternoon about sunset, as Pa and Almanzo were coming back from searching for the lost boy, they came by this place and stopped for a moment. The homesteader and his family had been gathering boards and bits of lumber that the storm had dropped, and he was figuring how much more he would have to get to build them some kind of shelter.

While they stood considering this, one of the children noticed a small dark object high in the clear sky overhead. It did not look like a bird, but it appeared to be growing larger. They all watched it. For some time it fell slowly towards them, and they saw that it was a door. It came gently down before them. It was the front door of this man's vanished claim shanty.

It was in perfect condition, not injured at all, not even scratched. The wonder was, where it had been all those hours, and that it had come slowly down from a clear sky, directly over the place where the claim shanty had been.

'I never saw a man more chirked up than he was,' said Pa. 'Now he doesn't have to buy a door for his new shanty. It even came back with the hinges on it.'

They were all amazed. In all their lives, none of them had ever heard of a stranger thing than the return of that door. It was awesome to think how far or how high it must have gone in air during all those hours.

'It's a queer country out here,' Pa said. 'Strange things happen.'

'Yes,' said Ma. 'I'm thankful that so far they don't happen to us.'

That next week Pa heard in town that the bodies of the lost boy and the mules had been found the next day. Every bone in them was broken. The clothing had been stripped from the boy and the harness from the mules. No scrap of clothing or harness was ever found.

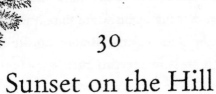

30

Sunset on the Hill

One Sunday Laura did not go driving, for it was Mary's last day at home. She was going back to college next day.

The weather was so very warm that at breakfast Ma said she believed she would not go to church. Carrie and Grace would stay at home with her, while Laura and Mary went with Pa in the wagon.

Pa was waiting for them when they came from the bedroom, ready to go.

Laura wore again her sprigged, pale pink lawn dress and her new hat with the ostrich tips now sewed on tightly.

Mary's dress was a blue lawn with small white flowers scattered over it. Her hat was a white straw sailor with a blue ribbon band. Beneath its brim at the back her hair was a great mass of twisted gold, and golden bangs curled richly on her forehead, above her eyes as blue as her ribbons.

Pa looked at them for a moment. His eyes shone and his voice was proud as he exclaimed in mock dismay, 'Jerusalem Crickets, Caroline! I'm not spruce enough to beau two such fine-looking young ladies to church!'

He looked nice, too, in his black suit with the black velvet collar on the coat, his white shirt, and dark blue tie.

The wagon was waiting. Before he dressed Pa had combed and brushed the two farm horses and spread a clean horse blanket on the wagon seat. The team drowsed while Pa carefully helped Mary up over the wheel, then gave his hand to Laura. Over their laps they spread the light dust robe and carefully Laura tucked its edge well around her full-gathered tucked lawn skirt. Then in the sunshine and the hot wind, slowly they rode to church.

It was so crowded that morning that they could not find three empty places together. So Pa went forward to sit with the greybeards in the amen corner, while Laura and Mary sat side by side near the middle of the church.

Reverend Brown was preaching earnestly and Laura was wishing that with so much sincerity he could say something interesting, when she saw a plump kitten straying up the aisle. Idly she watched it pounce and play, until it wandered on to the platform and stood arching its back and rubbing against the side of the pulpit. As its round, kitten eyes looked at the congregation, Laura believed she could hear its purring.

Then, at her side in the aisle, a small dog passed, trotting briskly. It was a little black-and-tan, with slender legs and a perky short tail, and its quick, businesslike trot was natural to it. It was not seeking anyone nor going anywhere, but merely sight-seeing in the church, until it spied the kitten. For an instant the little dog stiffened, then with a firecracker explosion of shrill yaps, it leaped.

The kitten's back rose in an arch, its tail swelled, and in a flash it vanished from Laura's view.

The strange thing was that it seemed to vanish utterly. There was no chase, and the little dog was silent. Reverend Brown went on preaching. Laura barely had time to wonder when she felt a slight swaying of her hoops, and looking down she saw the tip of the kitten's tail slide out of sight beneath the pink lawn ruffle.

The kitten had taken refuge under her hoops, and now it began climbing up inside them, clutching and clawing its way from wire to wire. Laura felt an impulse to laugh, but she controlled it and sat solemn as a judge. Then the little dog passed anxiously, peering and sniffing in search of the kitten, and a sudden vision of what would happen if he found it made Laura shake from head to foot with suppressed laughter.

She could feel her ribs swelling against her corsets and her cheeks puffing out and her throat choking. Mary did not know what amused Laura, but felt that she was laughing and pushed her elbow against Laura's side, whispering, 'Behave yourself.'

Laura shook all the harder and felt her face growing purple. Her hoops kept swaying under her skirts as the kitten cautiously crept down them again. Its little whiskered nose and eyes peeped from beneath the pink ruffle, then, seeing nothing of the dog, it popped out suddenly and scampered down the aisle towards the door. Laura listened, but she heard no yapping so she knew that the kitten had escaped.

On the way home Mary said, 'Laura, I am surprised at you. Will you never learn to behave yourself properly in church?'

Laura laughed until she cried, while Mary still sat disapproving and Pa wanted to know what had happened.

'No, Mary, I never will,' Laura said at last, wiping her eyes. 'You might as well give me up as a hopeless case.' Then she told them, and even Mary had to smile.

Sunday dinner and the afternoon passed quietly in family talk, and when the sun was sinking Mary and Laura took their last walk together to the top of the low hill to see the sunset.

'I never see things so well with anyone else,' Mary said. 'And when I come again you will not be here.'

'No, but you will come to see me where I am,' Laura answered. 'There will be two homes for you to visit.'

'But these sunsets . . .' Mary began, and Laura interrupted.

'The sun will set on Almanzo's farm, too, I hope,' she teased. 'There is no little hill there, but there are ten whole acres of little trees. We shall walk among them and you shall see them. There are cottonwoods, of course, but besides, there are box elders and maples and willows. If they live, they will be a beautiful grove. Not just a windbreak around the house, like Pa's, but real little woods.'

'It will be strange, to see these prairies wooded,' Mary said.

'Everything changes,' said Laura.

'Yes.' They were silent a little while, then Mary said, 'I wish I could be at your wedding. Don't you want to put it off till next June?'

Slowly Laura answered, 'No, Mary. I'm eighteen now and I've taught three terms of school, that's one more than Ma taught. I don't want to teach any more. I want to be settled this winter in our own home.

'It will be just the ceremony, anyway,' she added. 'Pa could not afford a wedding and I would not want the folks to go to any expense. When you come back next summer my house will be all ready for you to visit me in.'

'Laura,' Mary said. 'I'm sorry about the organ. If I'd known . . . but I did want to see Blanche's home, too, and it was near, and saved Pa the cost of my railroad journey, and I didn't realize that anything would ever change, here at home. I felt it was always here, to come back to.'

'It really is, Mary,' Laura told her. 'And don't feel bad at all about the organ. Just remember what a nice time you had at Blanche's. I am glad you went, truly I am, and so is Ma. She said so at the time.'

'Did she?' Mary's face lighted. Then Laura told her

what Ma had said of being glad that she was having good times while she was young, to remember. The sun was sinking now, and she told how its glory of crimson and gold flamed upon the sky and faded to rose and grey.

'Let's go back to the house now,' Mary said. 'I can feel the change in the air.'

They stood a moment longer with hands clasped, facing the west, then slowly they walked down the slope past the stable.

'Time passes so quickly now,' said Mary. 'Do you remember when the winter was so long, it seemed that summer would never come. And then in summertime, winter was so long ago we almost forgot what it was like?'

'Yes, and what good times we had when we were little,' Laura answered. 'But maybe the times that are coming will be even better. You never know.'

31
Wedding Plans

As always, Mary's going away made an emptiness in the house. The next morning Ma said briskly, 'We will get at your sewing now, Laura. Busy hands are a great help to being cheerful.'

So Laura brought the muslins, Ma cut them out, and the airy sitting room filled with the sewing machine's hum and the busy cheerfulness of Ma's and Laura's sewing together.

'I have an idea for making the sheets,' said Laura. 'I'm not going to sew those long seams down the middle with over-and-over stitch by hand. If I lap the edges flat and sew with the machine down the centre, I do believe they'll be smooth enough and even more serviceable.'

'It may well be,' said Ma. 'Our grandmothers would turn in their graves, but after all, these are modern times.'

All the white sewing was quickly done on the machine. Laura brought out the dozens of yards of white thread lace that she had knitted and crocheted, and like magic the machine's flashing needle stitched the lace edgings to the open ends of the pillow cases, the throats and wrists of the high-necked, long-sleeved nightgowns, the necks and armholes of the chemises, and the leg-bands of the drawers.

Busily working with the white goods, Ma and Laura discussed Laura's dresses.

'My brown poplin openwork dress is good as new,' Laura said. 'And my pink sprigged lawn *is* new. What more do I need?'

'You need a black dress,' Ma answered decisively. 'I think every woman should have one nice black dress. We'd better go to town Saturday and get the goods. A cashmere, I think. Cashmere wears well, and it is always dressy for all but the very hottest days of summer. Then when that dress is out of the way, you must get something pretty for your wedding.'

'There will be plenty of time,' Laura said. In the rush of summer work, Almanzo had little time to work on the house. He had taken Ma and Laura one Sunday to see its skeleton of studding standing by the piles of lumber, back from the road behind the grove of little sapling trees.

There were to be three rooms, the large room, a bedroom, and a pantry, with a lean-to over the back door besides. But after Laura had seen how these were planned, Almanzo did not take her to look at the house again. 'Leave it to me,' he said. 'I'll get a roof over it before snow flies.'

So they made their long Sunday drives to the twin lakes or to Spirit Lake and beyond.

On Monday morning Ma unfolded the soft lengths of sooty black cashmere and carefully fitting the newspaper pattern pieces to the goods so that none would be wasted, she cut confidently with her large shears. She cut out and pinned together all the skirt gores, the bodice pieces, and the sleeves. After dinner the sewing machine was threaded with black, and started.

It was humming steadily, late that afternoon, and Laura was basting the pieces of cambric lining to the cashmere pieces, when she looked up from her work and saw Almanzo driving up to the house. Something had happened, she was sure, or he would not come on Tuesday. She hurried to the door, and he said, 'Come for a little drive. I want to talk to you.'

Putting on her sunbonnet, Laura went with him.

'What is it?' she asked as Barnum and Skip trotted away.

'It is just this,' Almanzo said earnestly. 'Do you want a big wedding?'

She looked at him in amazement, that he should have come to ask her that, when they would see each other next Sunday. 'Why do you ask?' she inquired.

'If you don't, would you be willing and could you be ready to be married the last of this week, or the first of next?' he asked even more anxiously. 'Don't answer till I tell you why. When I was back in Minnesota last winter, my sister Eliza started planning a big church wedding for us. I told her we didn't want it, and to give up the idea. This morning I got a letter; she has not changed her mind. She is coming out here with my mother, to take charge of our wedding.'

'Oh, *no*!' Laura said.

'You know Eliza,' said Almanzo. 'She's headstrong, and she always was bossy, but I could handle this, if it was only Eliza. My mother's different, she's more like your mother; you'll like her. But Eliza's got Mother's heart set on our having a big church wedding, and if they are here before we're married, I don't see how I can tell Mother, "No." I don't want that kind of a wedding, and I can't afford what it would cost me. What do you think about it?'

There was a little silence while Laura thought. Then she said quietly, 'Pa can't afford to give me that kind of a wedding, either. I would like a little longer to get my things made. If we are married so soon I won't have a wedding dress.'

'Wear the one you have on. It is pretty,' Almanzo urged.

Laura could not help laughing. 'This is a calico work dress. I couldn't possibly!' Then she sobered, 'But Ma and I are making one that I could wear.'

'Then will you, say the last of this week?'

Laura was silent again. Then she summoned all her courage and said, 'Almanzo, I must ask you something. Do you want me to promise to obey you?'

Soberly he answered, 'Of course not. I know it is in the wedding ceremony, but it is only something that women say. I never knew one that did it, nor any decent man that wanted her to.'

'Well, I am not going to say I will obey you,' said Laura.

'Are you for women's rights, like Eliza?' Almanzo asked in surprise.

'No,' Laura replied. 'I do not want to vote. But I can not make a promise that I will not keep, and, Almanzo, even if I tried, I do not think I could obey anybody against my better judgement.'

'I'd never expect you to,' he told her. 'And there will be no difficulty about the ceremony, because Reverend Brown does not believe in using the word "obey".'

'He doesn't! Are you sure?' Laura had never been so surprised and so relieved, all at once.

'He feels very stongly about it,' Almanzo said. 'I have

heard him arguing for hours and quoting Bible texts against St Paul, on that subject. You know he is a cousin of John Brown of Kansas, and a good deal like him. Will it be all right, then? The last of this week, or early next?'

'Yes, if it is the only way to escape a big wedding,' said Laura. 'I will be ready the last of this week or the first of next, whichever you say.'

'If I can get the house finished, we'll say the last of this week,' Almanzo considered. 'If not, it will have to be next week. Let's say when the house is finished we will just drive to Reverend Brown's and be married quietly without any fuss. I'll take you home now and I may have time to get in a few more licks on the house yet tonight.'

At home again, Laura hesitated to tell of the plan. She felt that Ma would think the haste unseemly. Ma might say, 'Marry in haste, repent at leisure.' Yet they were not really marrying in haste. They had been going together for three years.

It was not until suppertime that Laura found courage to say that she and Almanzo had planned to be married so soon.

'We can't possibly get you a wedding dress made,' Ma objected.

'We can finish the black cashmere and I will wear that,' Laura answered.

'I do not like to think of your being married in black,'

said Ma. 'You know they say, "Married in black, you'll wish yourself back."'

'It will be new. I will wear my old sage-green poke bonnet with the blue silk lining, and borrow your little square gold pin with the strawberry in it, so I'll be wearing something old and something new, something borrowed and something blue,' Laura said cheerfully.

'I don't suppose there's any truth in these old sayings,' Ma consented.

Pa said, 'I think it is a sensible thing to do. You and Almanzo show good judgement.'

But Ma was not wholly satisfied yet. 'Let Reverend Brown come here. You can be married at home, Laura. We can have a nice little wedding here.'

'No, Ma, we couldn't have any kind of a wedding and not wait to have Almanzo's mother here,' Laura objected.

'Laura is right, and you think so yourself, Caroline,' said Pa.

'Of course I do,' Ma admitted.

32

'Haste to the Wedding'

Carrie and Grace eagerly offered to do all the housework, so that Ma and Laura could finish the cashmere, and every day that week they sewed as fast as they could. They made a tight-fitting basque, pointed at the bottom back and front, lined with black cambric lining and boned with whalebones on every seam. It had a high collar of cashmere. The sleeves were lined, too. They were long and plain and beautifully fitted, with a little fullness at the top but tight at the wrists. A shirring around each armhole, in front, made a graceful fullness over the breast, that was taken up by darts below. Small round black buttons buttoned the basque straight down the front.

The skirt just touched the floor all around. It fitted smoothly at the top, but was gored to fullness at the bottom. It was lined throughout with the cambric dress lining, and interlined with crinoline from the bottom to as high as Laura's shoes. The bottom of the skirt and the linings were turned under and the raw edges covered with dress braid, which Laura hemmed down by hand on both edges, so that no stitches showed on the right side.

There was no drive that Sunday. Almanzo came by for only a moment in his work clothes, to say that he was breaking the Sabbath by working on the house. It would be finished, he said, by Wednesday; so they could be married Thursday. He would come for Laura at ten o'clock Thursday morning, for the Reverend Brown was leaving town on the eleven o'clock train.

'Then better come over with your wagon, Wednesday, if you can make it, for Laura's things,' Pa told him. Almanzo said he would, and so it was settled, and with a smile to Laura he drove quickly away.

Tuesday morning Pa drove to town, and at noon he came back bringing Laura a present of a new trunk. 'Better put your things into it today,' he said.

With Ma's help, Laura packed her trunk that afternoon. Her old rag doll, Charlotte, with all her clothes carefully packed in a cardboard box, she put in the very bottom. Laura's winter clothes were laid in next, then her sheets and pillow cases and towels, her new white clothes and calico dresses, and her brown poplin. The pink lawn was carefully laid on top so that it would not be crushed. In the hatbox of the trunk's till, Laura put her new hat with the ostrich tips, and in the shallow till itself she had her knitting and crochet needles and worsted yarns.

Carrie brought Laura's glass box from the whatnot saying, 'I know you want this.'

Laura held the box in her hand, undecided. 'I hate to take this box away from Mary's. They shouldn't be separated,' she mused.

'See, I've moved my box closer to Mary's,' Carrie showed her. 'It doesn't look lonesome.' So Laura put her box carefully in the trunk till, among the soft yarns, where it could not be broken.

The trunk was packed, and Laura shut down the lid. Then Ma spread a clean, old sheet across the bed. 'You will want your quilt,' she said.

Laura brought her Dove-in-the-Window quilt that she had pieced as a little girl while Mary pieced a nine-patch. It had been kept carefully all the years since then. Ma laid it, folded, on the sheet, and upon it she placed two large, plump pillows.

'I want you to have these, Laura,' she said. 'You helped me save the feathers from geese that Pa shot on Silver Lake. They are good as new; I have been saving them for you. This red-and-white-checked tablecloth is like those I have always had; I thought it might make the new home more homelike if you saw it on your table,' and Ma laid the tablecloth, still in its paper wrapping, on the pillow. She drew the corners of the old sheet together over all, and tied them firmly. 'There, that will keep the dust out,' she said.

Almanzo came next morning with Barnum and Skip hitched to his wagon. He and Pa loaded the trunk and the pillow bundle into it. Then Pa said, 'Wait a minute, don't hurry away, I'll be back,' and he went into the house. For a moment or two all the others stood by the wagon, talking, and waiting for Pa to come from the door.

Then he came around the corner of the house, leading Laura's favourite young cow. She was fawn-coloured all over, and gentle. Quietly Pa tied her behind the wagon, then threw her picket rope into the wagon as he said, 'Her picket rope goes with her.'

'Oh, Pa!' Laura cried. 'Do you really mean I may take Fawn with me?'

'That is exactly what I do mean!' Pa said. 'Be a pity if you couldn't have one calf out of all you have helped to raise.'

Laura could not speak, but she gave Pa a look that thanked him.

'You think it is safe to tie her behind those horses?' Ma asked, and Almanzo assured her that it was safe, and said to Pa that he appreciated the gift of a cow.

Then turning to Laura he said, 'I'll be over in the morning at ten o'clock.'

'I will be ready,' Laura promised, but as she stood watching Almanzo drive away, she was unable to realize that tomorrow she would leave home. Try as she would, she could not think of going away tomorrow as meaning that she would not come back, as she had always come back from drives with Almanzo.

That afternoon the finished black cashmere was carefully pressed, and then Ma made a big, white cake. Laura helped her by beating the egg whites on a platter with a fork, until Ma said they were stiff enough.

'My arm is stiffer,' Laura ruefully laughed, rubbing her aching right arm.

'This cake must be just right,' Ma insisted. 'If you can't have a wedding party, at least you shall have a wedding dinner at home, and a wedding cake.'

After supper that night, Laura brought Pa's fiddle to him, and asked, 'Please, Pa, make some music.'

Pa took the fiddle from the box. He was a long time tuning it; then he must resin the bow carefully. At last he poised the bow above the fiddle strings and cleared his throat. 'What will you have, Laura?'

'Play for Mary first,' Laura answered. 'And then play all the old tunes, one after another, as long as you can.'

She sat on the doorstep and just inside the door Pa and Ma sat looking out over the prairie while Pa played 'Highland Mary'. Then while the sun was going down he played all the old tunes that Laura had known ever since she could remember.

The sun sank from sight, trailing bright banners after it. The colours faded, the land grew shadowy, the first star twinkled. Softly Carrie and Grace came to lean against

Ma. The fiddle sang on in the twilight.

It sang the songs that Laura knew in the Big Woods of Wisconsin, and the tunes that Pa had played by the campfires all across the plains of Kansas. It repeated the nightingale's song in the moonlight on the banks of the Verdigris River, then it remembered the days in the dugout on the banks of Plum Creek, and the winter evenings in the new house that Pa had built there. It sang of the Christmas on Silver Lake, and of springtime after the long Hard Winter.

Then the fiddle sounded a sweeter note and Pa's deep voice joined its singing.

> 'Once in the dear dead days beyond recall
> Ere on the world the mists began to fall,
> Out of the dreams that rose in happy
>   throng,
> Low to our hearts love sang an old sweet
>   song.
> And in the dusk where fell the firelight
>   gleam
> Softly it wove itself into our dream.
>
> Just a song at twilight, when the lights are
>   low
> And the flickering shadows softly come and
>   go,

'HASTE TO THE WEDDING'

Though the heart be weary, sad the day and
    long,
Still to us at twilight comes love's old song,
Comes love's old sweet song.

Even today we hear love's song of yore,
Deep in our hearts it swells forever more.
Footsteps may falter and weary grow the
    way,
Still we can hear it at the close of day,
So to the end when life's dim shadows fall,
Love will be found the sweetest song of all.'

Little Grey Home in the West

Laura was ready when Almanzo came. She was wearing her new black cashmere dress and her sage-green poke bonnet with the blue lining and the blue ribbon bow tied under her left ear. The soft black tips of her shoes barely peeped from beneath her flaring skirt as she walked.

Ma herself had pinned her square gold brooch with the imbedded strawberry at Laura's throat, against the bit of white lace that finished the collar of her dress.

'There!' Ma said. 'Even if your dress is black, you look perfect.'

Gruffly Pa said, 'You'll do, Half-Pint.'

Carrie brought a fine white handkerchief, edged with lace matching the lace on Laura's collar. 'I made it for you,' she said. 'It looks nice in your hand, against your black dress.'

Grace just stood near and admired. Then Almanzo came, and they all watched at the door while Laura and Almanzo drove away.

Once Laura spoke. 'Does Reverend Brown know we are coming'

Almanzo said, 'I saw him on my way over. He will not use the word, "obey".'

Mrs Brown opened the sitting-room door. Nervously she said that she would call Mr Brown, and asked them to sit down. She went into the bedroom and closed the door.

Laura and Almanzo sat waiting. In the centre of the sitting room a marble-topped table stood on a crocheted rag rug. On the wall was a large coloured picture of a woman clinging to a white cross planted on a rock, with lightning streaking the sky above her and huge waves dashing high around her.

The door of the other bedroom opened and Ida slipped in and sat down in a chair near the door. She gave Laura a frightened smile and then twisted her handkerchief in her lap and looked at it.

The kitchen door opened and a tall, thin young man quietly slipped into a chair. Laura supposed he was Elmer but she did not see him, for Reverend Brown came from the bedroom, thrusting his arms into his coat sleeves. He settled the coat collar to his neck and asked Laura and Almanzo to rise and stand before him.

So they were married.

Reverend Brown and Mrs Brown and Elmer shook their hands, and Almanzo quietly handed Reverend Brown a folded bill. Reverend Brown unfolded it, and at first did not understand that Almanzo meant to give him all of ten dollars. Ida squeezed Laura's hand and tried to speak, but choked; quickly she kissed Laura, slipped a soft little package into her hand, and ran out of the room.

Laura and Almanzo came out into the sun and wind. He helped her into the buggy and untied the horses. They drove back through town. Dinner was ready when they came back. Ma and the girls had moved the table into the sitting room, between the open door and the open windows. They had covered it with the best white tablecloth and set it with the prettiest dishes. The silver spoons in the spoon holder shone in the centre of the table and the steel knives and forks were polished until they were as bright.

As Laura hesitated shyly at the door, Carrie asked, 'What's that in your hand?'

Laura looked down. She was holding in her hand, with Carrie's handkerchief, the soft little package that Ida had given her. She said, 'Why, I don't know. Ida gave it to me.'

She opened the small tissue-paper package and unfolded the most beautiful piece of lace she had ever seen. It was a triangular fichu, of white silk lace, a pattern of lovely flowers and leaves.

'That will last you a lifetime, Laura,' Ma said, and Laura knew that she would always keep and treasure this lovely thing that Ida had given her.

Then Almanzo came from stabling the horses, and they all sat down to dinner.

It was one of Ma's delicious dinners, but all the food

tasted alike to Laura. Even the wedding cake was dry as sawdust in her mouth, for at last she realized that she was going away from home, that never would she come back to this home to stay. They all lingered at the table, for they knew that after dinner came the parting, but finally Almanzo said that it was time to go.

Laura put her bonnet on again, and went out to the buggy as Almanzo drove to the door. There were good-bye kisses and good wishes, while he stood ready to help her into the buggy. But Pa took her hand.

'You'll help her from now on, young man,' he said to Almanzo. 'But this time, I will.' Pa helped her into the buggy.

Ma brought a basket covered with a white cloth. 'Something to help make your supper,' she said and her lips trembled. 'Come back soon, Laura.'

When Almanzo was lifting the reins, Grace came running with Laura's old slat sunbonnet. 'You forgot this!' she called, holding it up. Almanzo checked the horses while Laura took the sunbonnet. As the horses started again, Grace called anxiously after them, 'Remember, Laura, Ma says if you don't keep your sunbonnet on, you'll be brown as an Indian!'

So everyone was laughing when Laura and Almanzo drove away.

They drove over the road they had travelled so many times, across the neck of Big Slough, around the corner by Pearson's livery barn, up Main Street and across the railroad tracks, then out on the road towards the new house on Almanzo's tree claim.

It was a silent drive until almost the end, when for the

first time that day Laura saw the horses. She exclaimed, 'Why, you are driving Prince and Lady!'

'Prince and Lady started this,' Almanzo said. 'So I thought they'd like to bring us home. And here we are.'

The tracks of his wagon and buggy wheels had made a perfect half-circle drive curving into the grove of little sapling trees before the house. There the house sat, and it was neatly finished with siding and smoothly painted a soft grey. Its front door was comfortably in the middle, and two windows gave the whole house a smiling look. On the doorstep lay a large, brown shepherd dog, that rose and politely wagged to Laura as the buggy stopped.

'Hello, Shep!' Almanzo said. He helped Laura down and unlocked the door. 'Go in while I put up the horses,' he told her.

Just inside the door she stood and looked. This was the large room. Its walls were neatly plastered a soft white. At its far end stood a drop-leaf table, covered with Ma's red-checked tablecloth. A chair sat primly at either end of it. Beside it was a closed door.

In the centre of the long wall at Laura's left, a large window let in the sunshine. Companionably placed at either side of it, two rocking chairs faced each other. Beside the one nearer Laura stood a small round table, and above it a hanging lamp was suspended from the ceiling. Someone could sit there in the evening and read a paper, while in the other chair someone could knit.

The window beside the front door let still more sunny light into the pleasant room.

Two closed doors were in the other long wall. Laura opened the one nearer her, and saw the bedroom. Her Dove-in-the-Window quilt was spread upon the wide bed, and her two feather pillows stood plumply at the head of it. At its foot, across the whole length of the partition, was a wide shelf higher than Laura's head, and from its edge a prettily flowered calico curtain hung to the floor. It made a perfect clothes closet. Against the wall under the front window stood Laura's trunk.

She had seen all this quickly. Now she took off her poke bonnet and laid it on the shelf. She opened her trunk and took out a calico dress and apron. Taking off her black cashmere, she hung it carefully in the curtain closet, then slipped into the blue calico dress and tied on the crisply ruffled, pink apron. She went into the front room as Almanzo came into it through the door by the drop-leaf table.

'All ready for work, I see!' he said gaily, as he set Ma's basket on the chair near him. 'Guess I'd better get ready for my work, too.' He turned at the bedroom door to say, 'Your Ma told me to open your bundle and spread things around.'

'I'm glad you did,' Laura told him.

She looked through the door by the table. There was the lean-to. Almanzo's bachelor cook-stove was set up there, and pots and frying pan hung on the walls. There was a window, and a back door that looked out at the stable beyond some little trees.

Laura returned to the front room. She took up Ma's basket, and opened the last door. She knew it must be the pantry door, but she stood in surprise and then in delight, looking at that pantry. All one wall was covered with shelves and drawers, and a broad shelf was under a large window at the pantry's far end.

She took Ma's basket to that shelf, and opened it. There was a loaf of Ma's good bread, a ball of butter, and what had been left of the wedding cake. She left it all on the shelf while she investigated the pantry.

One whole long wall was shelved from the ceiling halfway down. The upper shelves were empty, but on the lowest was a glass lamp, Almanzo's bachelor dishes, and two pans of milk, with empty pans near. At the end, where this shelf was above the window shelf in the corner, stood a row of cans of spices.

Beneath this shelf were many drawers of different sizes. Directly below the spices, and above the window shelf, were two rather narrow drawers. Laura found that one was almost full of white sugar, the other of brown sugar. How handy!

Next, a deep drawer was full of flour, and smaller ones held graham flour and corn meal. You could stand at the window shelf and mix up anything, without stirring a step.

Outside the window was the great, blue sky, and the leafy little trees.

Another deep drawer was filled with towels and tea towels. Another held two tablecloths and some napkins. A shallow one held knives and forks and spoons.

Beneath all these drawers there was space for a tall, stoneware churn and dasher, and empty space for other things as they should come.

In a wide drawer of the bottom row was only a crust of bread and half a pie. Here Laura put Ma's loaf of bread and the wedding cake. She cut a piece from the ball of butter, put it on a small plate, and placed it beside the bread. Then she pushed the drawer shut.

By the iron ring fastened in the pantry floor, she knew there was a trap door. She straightened the ring up, and pulled. The trap door rose, and rested against the pantry wall opposite the shelves. There, beneath where it had been, the cellar stairs went down.

Carefully covering the ball of butter, Laura carried it down the stairs into the cool, dark cellar, and set it on a hanging shelf that swung from the ceiling. She heard steps overhead, and as she came up the cellar stairs she heard Almanzo calling her name.

'I thought you were lost in this big house!' he said.

'I was putting the butter down cellar so it would keep cool,' said Laura.

'Like your pantry?' he asked her, and she thought how

many hours he must have worked, to put up all those shelves and to make and fit those many drawers.

'Yes,' she said.

'Then let's go look at Lady's big little colt. I want you to see the horses in their stalls, and the place I have fixed for your cow. She's picketed out to grass now, just out of reach of the young trees.' Almanzo led the way through the lean-to and outdoors.

They explored the long stable and the yard beyond it. Almanzo showed her the new haystacks on the north, to shelter the yard and stable when the winter winds came. Laura petted the horses and the colt, and Shep as he followed close at their heels. They looked at the little maples and box elders and willows and cottonwoods.

Quickly, the afternoon was gone. It was time for chores and supper.

'Don't build a fire,' Almanzo told her. 'Set out that bread and butter your mother gave us; I'll milk Fawn, and we'll have bread and new milk for supper.'

'And cake,' Laura reminded him.

When they had eaten supper and washed the few dishes, they sat on the front doorstep as evening came. They heard Prince blow out his breath, whoof! as he lay down on his bed of clean hay in the stable. They saw the dim bulk of Fawn on the grass, where she lay chewing her cud and resting. Shep lay at their feet; already he was half Laura's dog.

Laura's heart was full of happiness. She knew she need never be homesick for the old home. It was so near that she could go to it whenever she wished, while she and Almanzo made the new home in their own little house.

All this was theirs; their own horses, their own cow, their own claim. The many leaves of their little trees rustled softly in the gentle breeze.

Twilight faded as the little stars went out and the moon rose and floated upward. Its silvery light flooded the sky and the prairie. The winds that had blown whispering over the grasses all the summer day now lay sleeping, and quietness brooded over the moon-drenched land.

'It is a wonderful night,' Almanzo said.

'It is a beautiful world,' Laura answered, and in memory she heard the voice of Pa's fiddle and the echo of a song,

'Golden years are passing by,
These happy, golden years.'

Inside the cosy little house in the
Big Woods lives the Ingalls family:
Ma, Pa, Mary, Laura and baby Carrie.
Outside the little house, in the snow
and the cold, are the wild animals.

This is the classic tale of how they live together,
mostly in harmony, but sometimes in fear . . .

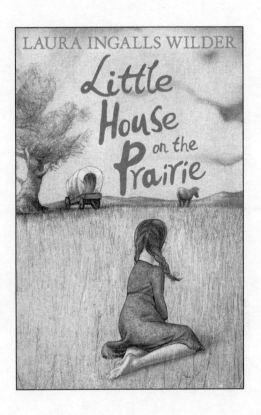

The sun-kissed prairie stretches out around the Ingalls family, smiling its welcome after their long, hard journey across America.

But looks can be deceiving, and they soon find that they must share the land with wild bears and Indians.

Will there be enough land for all of them?

Read all the books in the

Little House on the Prairie series: